# THE BAYOU BULLETIN

## Advertisement

Remy Delacroix's

### WILLOW ISLAND
### SWAMP TOURS

Explore one of Louisiana's most
beautiful swamps featuring resident
and migratory wildlife.

— Professionally narrated boat tours offered
daily, year-round.
— Group rates available.
— Gift Shop featuring native crafts.

For additional information and
reservations, call
(504) 555-5217
102 Cypress Drive
Bayou Beltane, Louisiana 70451

D0051251

Barbara Colley is acknowledged
as the author of this work.

ISBN 0-373-82563-3

FINDING KENDALL

# DELTA JUSTICE

# Finding Kendall

## ANNE LOGAN

## Harlequin Books

TORONTO • NEW YORK • LONDON
AMSTERDAM • PARIS • SYDNEY • HAMBURG
STOCKHOLM • ATHENS • TOKYO • MILAN
MADRID • WARSAW • BUDAPEST • AUCKLAND

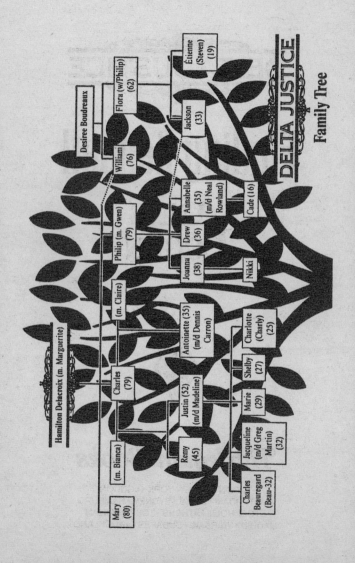

# DELTA JUSTICE
## Family Tree

Hamilton Delacroix (m. Marguerite)

Desiree Boudreaux

Mary (80)

(m. Bianca)

Charles (79)

(m. Claire)

Philip (m. Gwen) (79)

William (76)

Flora (w/Philip) (62)

Remy (45)

Justin (52) (m/d Madeline)

Antoinette (35) (m/d Dennis Carron)

Joanna (38)

Drew (36)

Annabelle (35) (m/d Neal Rowland)

Jackson (33)

Étienne (Steven) (19)

Charles Beauregard (Beau-32)

Jacqueline (m/d Greg Martin) (32)

Marie (29)

Shelby (27)

Charlotte (Charly) (25)

Nikki

Cade (16)

# CAST OF CHARACTERS

**Remy Delacroix**—ex-cop who now lives in the bayou and runs a swamp tour business.

**Kendall Delaney, a.k.a. Jane Doe**—works for the Louisiana Department of Environmental Standards and finds herself under Remy's wing after an accident in the swamp.

**Philip Delacroix**—Remy's uncle, who's in cahoots with Kendall's corrupt boss, Don Talbot.

**Charly Delacroix**—Remy's niece, and a member of the New Orleans police academy.

**Desiree Boudreaux**—Remy's good friend and neighbor, who concocts healing herbal remedies from the flora from the swamp.

**Della Delaney**—Kendall Delaney's invalid mother.

**Jake Trahan**—chief of police of Bayou Beltane, and one of the few men Remy trusts.

**Claudia Landry**—Remy's loyal employee at the swamp tour gift shop.

Dear Reader,

I considered being invited to participate in Harlequin's exciting DELTA JUSTICE series both an honor and a privilege—an honor to be included in such a wonderful project and a privilege to work with such talented editors and writers.

I was born in Louisiana and have lived there all my life. I think my home state is unique—one of the most fascinating in the nation. I was thrilled that it was chosen to showcase this terrific series about the Delacroix family.

As for my own family, my great-grandmother was a Cherokee Indian from Louisiana who used herbal remedies for just about everything, so the character of Desiree came naturally to me. Also, I've always loved to read stories involving danger and suspense. In fact, the first book I ever attempted to write was a romantic suspense story about a woman who had amnesia. Then many years and published books later, along came DELTA JUSTICE and *Finding Kendall*. Wow! Did I ever have fun with it! You can understand why this book is special to me.

Louisiana is famous for its spicy Cajun cuisine, its music and wonderful jazz festival. People here really know how to enjoy themselves! My dearest wish is that you have as much fun reading *Finding Kendall* as I did writing it. So, as we say here, *Laissez les bon temps rouler!* (Let the good times roll!).

Sincerely,

Anne Logan

# CHAPTER ONE

REMY DELACROIX stood over the woman sprawled in the dark gumbo mud. She was as still as death, and as he stared down at her pale face, for a moment it was déjà vu....

*Julie...lying in a New Orlean's gutter...blood gushing from her body....*

He shook his head. Though young and obviously beautiful, this woman was not Julie.

Willow Island was in the middle of the vast, peaceful Louisiana swamp, a far cry from the mean streets of New Orleans.

He dropped to one knee beside her.

Judging from the dried mud on her blouse and the dried blood caked in her hair at her right temple, Remy guessed she'd been there awhile. He reached out. Her skin was cool to the touch, but not deathly cold.

He pressed his fingers to the side of her neck, searching for the steady throb that would indicate life, prove that blood still flowed through her veins. "Where is it?" he muttered. "Come on. Be there, dammit!"

Then he found it—a pulse—strong despite her condition.

He sighed with relief and moved his fingers to the

spot on her head that was caked with blood. Gingerly probing the area, he uncovered a small gash, the kind that he knew from experience was usually caused by a blow, not a fall. As he stared at it, the skin on the back of his neck started to prickle.

Remy narrowed his eyes and quickly glanced around. Had someone knocked her unconscious? Had she been purposely left to die on the wild, remote island? Though it was possible she might have accidentally slipped and fallen, there weren't any jagged rocks or broken tree limbs nearby, nothing hard enough to cause an injury like the one on her head.

More wary and alert than before, he turned his attention back to the woman. She was dressed casually in khaki shorts, a loose cotton blouse and walking shoes. He could see no other signs of injury, except for a few mosquito bites…and her right arm.

"Damn!" Gingerly, he examined the arm, which was twisted at an odd angle. The bruising and swelling meant there was more than a good possibility that it was broken.

"Now what?" he muttered. He had a walkie-talkie in his boat, but the sun had long since disappeared behind the moss-draped cedars, and most of the birds had already gone to roost. Soon twilight would fade into night, and with the cool night temperatures came the foggy mist that hung suspended above the water. Disorienting enough in bright sunshine, the swamp became almost impossible to navigate in a fog. One wrong turn in the intricate system of waterways and even the most experienced person could wander for hours. No one in his right mind would venture into the swamp after dark even if Remy called for help, and there wouldn't be time to reach the shore for medical attention before the fog closed in. There was barely enough time to reach his houseboat.

He shook his head. "No choice at all. I sure as hell can't leave you here for the gators and mosquitoes."

Remy made a quick trip back to his motorboat, where he kept a spare blanket and a first aid kit. Using the blanket and some life jackets, he prepared a makeshift bed in the bottom of the aluminum craft then returned for the woman.

He tried his best to be gentle as he immobilized her arm, but even in her unconscious state he could tell from the pinched expression on her face that the slightest movement caused her pain.

"Sorry, sweetheart, I'm afraid this is going to hurt, too," he said, lifting her in his arms. Immediately he realized that the woman's looks were deceptive—despite her slim, feminine appearance, she was solidly built. She probably weighed about one hundred and thirty pounds.

Remy took one last look around for anything that might give a clue to her identity but found nothing. No doubt if she'd had a purse or a tote bag, whoever had assaulted her had taken it.

Once his patient was settled in the boat and wrapped in the blanket, Remy gunned the motor and headed for open water. It was a good fifteen minutes to his houseboat even in daylight, and he was seriously worried about the woman going into shock or worse.

By the time he finally rounded the last curve in

the bayou it was almost dark. Up ahead he spotted a small skiff tied at his pier. Desiree Boudreaux.

"Thank God," he muttered. Even though he wondered what the old woman was doing out at this time of night, there was no one he'd rather have seen at the moment. Her healing skills, though unorthodox, were known far and wide around Bayou Beltane— as were her more occult pursuits.

Like a phantom, Desiree seemed to materialize out of the shadows as Remy maneuvered his boat alongside the pier. For as far back as he could remember, she had always looked the same. There was an exotic, almost otherworldly appearance about the tiny woman. Her face was a road map of fine lines etched by time, and her abundant, wavy hair was as gray as an old cypress. Today it was held back by a turquoise scarf that matched the colorful, loose-flowing dress she wore.

"Ah, Remy, what have you got there?" she asked, her slight Cajun accent more pronounced than usual. She peered down at the boat. "Quite a catch, even for you," she cackled in a raspy voice.

Used to her ways, Remy ignored her teasing as he tied the boat securely to the pier. Lately Desiree had become obsessed with finding him a woman, the last thing in the world he wanted or needed. Desiree was always telling him that each of God's creatures needed a mate. *That's just nature's way,* she would drawl.

"I found her on Willow Island," he explained as he carefully lifted the unconscious woman in his arms and stepped onto the dock. "She's hurt—needs medical attention—but since I didn't relish wandering around lost in the swamp tonight, the only thing left to do was bring her home with me until morning. Would you take a look at her?''

The old woman nodded. "Take her inside.''

Moments later, Remy eased the patient onto his bed. She was still pale and had that pinched expression that he figured meant she was in pain.

"Well, are you gonna stand there all day gawking or are you gonna move out of the way and let me look at her?'' Desiree nudged him aside, and if Remy hadn't known better, he'd swear that the heat he felt crawling up his neck was from embarrassment. He hadn't realized that he'd been "gawking'' at the woman.

"I'll need the first aid kit, a pan of warm water, a washcloth, some bandages and something I can use for a splint,'' Desiree said as she leaned over the bed and lifted one of the woman's eyelids with her thumb. "I'll also need the green tackle box in my boat. Be careful you don't drop it and spill everything.'' She ran her fingers along the woman's injured arm.

Reluctantly Remy turned away to do Desiree's bidding. It wasn't that he didn't trust her—he did— but for reasons he couldn't explain, he was finding it hard to let the injured woman out of his sight.

*You discovered her, so you feel responsible,* he told himself as he headed for Desiree's boat.

The green tackle box was wedged in between two others—one blue and one gray—in the bottom of the small skiff. Remy knew that each tackle box contained specific items—the green one, medicinal herbs, the blue one, fishing tackle. And though he'd never actually seen inside the gray one, he suspected it contained ingredients Desiree and her daughter, Flora, used for their voodoo rituals, gris-gris and spells.

Remy took the green tackle box to Desiree, then set about gathering the other items she had requested. When he entered the bedroom again, he came to a dead halt just inside the doorway. Desiree had stripped off the woman's blouse, and except for the sheer, lacy bra she wore, she was bare from the waist up.

At the unexpected sight of her flawless skin, her feminine curves, he found it took every ounce of willpower he possessed to keep from really "gawking," and he suddenly felt like the worst kind of voyeur for having such a response, considering the circumstances.

"I don't think the arm is as bad as it looks," Desiree said when he deposited the items he'd collected on the bedside table. She glanced up at him. "But this head wound was no accident."

"Yeah, I thought the same thing."

"So?"

Remy shrugged. "So I'm hoping she can shed some light on the matter when she wakes up. She *will* wake up, won't she?"

Desiree turned back to tend the woman. "She'll wake up when she's good and ready. Some just take longer to come around than others. It's the body's way of dealing with things." Desiree opened the first aid kit and took out gauze and antiseptic lotion. "But for now, I need to clean that cut."

Still uncomfortable with his earlier inappropriate

reaction, Remy watched as Desiree wiped the dried blood from the woman's head wound. She was a blonde, he belatedly realized, and the wound seemed oddly obscene against the pale gold of her hair. The longer he watched, the more his fingers itched to snatch the antiseptic-soaked gauze from the old woman and do it himself.

Remy balled his hands into fists. What was it about the woman that was making him feel so...so territorial? he wondered. He didn't know her, had never laid eyes on her until he'd found her on Willow Island. And as he tried to convince himself that he was just concerned—no more or no less than he would be for anyone else in her situation—he chose to ignore the irritating voice inside his head that called him a liar.

Once Desiree had applied antibiotic ointment and a bandage to the head wound, she focused her attention on her patient's arm. "I don't think it's broken clear through. I think maybe it's just cracked below the elbow."

As the healer's deft fingers probed the bruised area, for the first time since he'd found her, the woman actually groaned, and Remy almost came unglued. "You're hurting her!" he exclaimed.

Desiree shrugged and continued her probing. "It's going to get a lot worse before it gets better," she said. "Just be glad she isn't conscious."

During the following minutes, Remy actually felt queasy as he watched Desiree set the woman's broken arm and bind it.

Once she'd finished, she picked up the woman's muddy blouse from the floor. "This is too dirty to put back on her.'' She tossed it to Remy. ''Get me one of your shirts—a clean one—and put this in water to soak.''

While she dressed the woman in his shirt, Remy took care of the blouse. When he returned, Desiree thrust a washcloth at him.

''Here. Wipe that dirt off her face and cool her off with this while I prepare her a drink. Hmm... something to ease her discomfort, I think, but something that won't entice her to keep sleeping.'' Desiree picked up the green tackle box, and with a thoughtful expression deepening the wrinkles etched in her forehead, she glided out of the room.

Taking care not to jar the woman, Remy eased down onto the edge of the bed. He rinsed the cloth in the basin of water and, turning to the patient, gently blotted her face, cleaning the last of the mud from her cheek and hairline.

Again he rinsed the cloth, then squeezed out the excess water and laid it across her forehead.

For long seconds he studied the face beneath the edge of the washcloth. Her ashen skin was smooth, almost flawless. Her long eyelashes were just a shade darker than her hair, and her pale lips were full....

*She's young,* he thought, suddenly feeling every one of his own forty-five years. She might be in her early thirties....

''This should do the trick.''

Remy started at the sound of Desiree's voice, and it disconcerted him to realize he'd been so completely preoccupied that he hadn't heard her come into the room.

He needed air, he decided. Fresh air to clear his head.

When he stood and moved aside, Desiree took his place, dipped a spoon into a cup of dark liquid and slipped it between the woman's lips.

Mesmerized, Remy watched the stuff disappear into her mouth, leaving only a trace of a stain on her pale lips. Dragging his eyes away, he turned and left the room.

Outside on the dock, he stared up at the full moon, a blurry globe just visible through the low-lying fog. The air was heavy with the earthy scents of the marsh, but no matter how tranquil the night, or how many deep breaths he drew, Remy still couldn't get the woman or the circumstances of how he'd found her out of his mind.

"Remy?" Desiree's reedy voice called from the doorway.

"Yeah, over here," he answered.

"Just wondering where you got off to," the old woman said as she approached him. "I've done all I can for your woman now. Nothing else to do but wait for her to wake up."

Something about the way Desiree said "your woman" gave Remy a jolt.

"You said you found her on Willow Island?" she continued. "That's not exactly on your way home. What were you doing over that way?"

Remy propped his hip against the railing that ran along one side of the dock and crossed his arms over his chest. "I saw more signs of poaching the other day over near Cypress Island, so I decided to take some time off and see if I could catch whoever's doing it red-handed.'' He shrugged one shoulder. ''I came close, but no brass ring, so I decided to call it a day. On my way back, I spotted one of my rental boats floating loose around the north side of Willow Island. Since no one was in it, I figured that whoever had rented it hadn't tied it securely and had gotten himself stranded. I towed it in and found her while I was searching the island.''

''You're not thinking that she's your poacher, eh?''

''The thought did cross my mind, but...'' He shook his head. ''Not really. I don't know who she is, but I've never heard of a woman poacher. Besides, the bastard I'm after wouldn't be stupid enough to *rent* a boat, especially one of mine.''

''So what do you think she was doing out there? And who did this to her?''

''I just don't know. Not yet, anyway.''

Desiree's questions hung in the air. They were the same questions that had been nagging him since he'd found the woman. Then suddenly, like a flash of lightning, it hit him. The survey markers. Could she have something to do with the survey markers he'd been finding in the swamp the last few months? He frowned. Even if she was connected to the mysterious markers in some way, that wouldn't explain why someone had attacked her and left her for dead. Remy's frown deepened into a scowl. Bayou Beltane was a small community, one of the safest places in south Louisiana to live and raise a family.

Four years ago, he'd needed a safe place to run to, a place to heal and forget that he'd ever been a New Orleans police detective. He'd found what he needed in the swamp. With Desiree's urging and encouragement, and despite the strident disapproval of his family, especially his father, he'd also found that he truly enjoyed his newfound vocation as a swamp-tour guide. As a boy, he'd always loved exploring the rich wetlands of the Mississippi Delta, filled with so many birds and other wildlife. Even then the swamp had been a refuge from his overpowering family, and now he took pride in showing the natural beauty to tourists.

But a poacher, an assault, possibly even an attempted murder... The idea of his sanctuary being tainted made his blood boil.

"Remy?" Desiree reached out and touched his arm to get his attention. Squinting her eyes, she peered up at him for long seconds. It was a look he recognized, the piercing scrutiny that made him feel as if the old woman knew exactly what was on his mind.

"No place is perfect," she said quietly. "Even the Garden of Eden had its snake. Once she wakes up, perhaps then you will have your answers."

Remy shook his head. "How do you do that? How do you always seem to know what I'm thinking?"

"I only do what comes natural. You're like a son to me, and what mother doesn't know her own son?"

*What comes natural, indeed,* he mused. Maybe the rumors were true after all. Maybe among her many talents, Desiree really was a witch who could discern the very thoughts in a person's head.

A sly smile pulled at her thin lips, and once again he got the feeling that she knew exactly what he'd been thinking. "You should report this to the sheriff, you know," she said.

"No!" Remy glared at her. "No cops. My swamp, my problem. I'll take care of it."

She made a sound of dismay. "Ah, *mon garçon*, still so much bitterness after all this time. Not all authority is bad. Jake Trahan isn't like those others. You can trust him. Jake is a good man, an honorable man."

"Being honorable is a relative thing," Remy retorted. "Anyone can be corrupted if the stakes are high enough."

Before Desiree could start one of her lectures, he decided to change the subject. "Don't get me wrong. I'm glad you're here, but did you come by for a visit or did you have a specific reason for being out this time of the evening?"

"We'll speak of this other matter again," she promised, "but to answer your question, both. I mixed a new batch of tea and wanted your opinion before I sell it to my customers. It's a special mix to calm and soothe."

"Since when did you decide to make me your guinea pig?"

"Since your souvenir shop is where I intend to—how you say—ah, test-market my first batch?"

In spite of himself, Remy felt a grin pulling at his lips. "Ah-ha, the truth comes out."

"Then it's settled, hmm? I can sell my herbal tea at the souvenir shop?"

"Yeah, along with all that other stuff you fill the shelves with."

"Your tourists like my *stuff*, as you call it."

Remy couldn't argue with her logic. When he'd taken over the tour-guide business from the previous owner, the souvenir shop had been a losing proposition. But with hard work, a bit of creativity and the native crafts, spices and voodoo charms that Desiree supplied, it was now thriving.

The old woman reached out and squeezed his arm affectionately. "And now that we've got that settled, you can go check on our patient while I brew you a sample of my new tea." With that, she turned and disappeared into the shadows along the pier.

When Remy entered the bedroom, the first thing he noted was that color had returned to the woman's cheeks. She looked more peaceful, as if she was finally sleeping restfully. Whatever Desiree had given her seemed to be working.

Remy eased down on the edge of the bed again. Unable to help himself, he smoothed back a strand of silky blond hair from her face.

"Who are you, pretty lady?" he murmured. "And what were you doing out there in that swamp all alone?"

Not alone. Someone else had been there with her, someone who had possibly tried to kill her. But who?

"She should rest easier now," Desiree said as she entered the room and handed Remy a steaming cup of tea.

Remy would have preferred a good strong cup of coffee and chicory, but to humor the old woman, he took a sip of Desiree's new concoction. Actually, the stuff didn't taste half-bad, he thought, and nodded his approval.

"Lucky thing for her that you came along." Desiree reached in front of Remy and felt the sleeping woman's forehead. "No fever yet," she murmured thoughtfully, removing her hand. "That's a good sign."

She turned to Remy. "I don't like you chasing this poacher. It's too dangerous." She held up her hand when she saw the expression on his face. "Yes, I know. I'm just an old woman who worries too much, and you're a grown man who can take care of himself."

Remy grinned. "Thanks, anyway. It's nice to know someone cares." His grin faded. "There's something else I haven't mentioned yet." He set the cup on the bedside table. "I saw another one of those survey stakes," he explained. "Like the ones out on Cypress Island."

A frown of anxiety deepened the lines in the old woman's forehead. "What do you think they mean?"

"I'm not sure yet, but so far it seems that most of them are on Uncle Philip's half of the family property, and I have a strong suspicion that he's up to something."

Desiree's expression hardened. "Up to no good, as usual."

"Yeah, you're probably right," Remy agreed. "But of course, that depends on which side of the family you belong to."

"Well, me—I don't belong to either side, but I've seen a lot in my ninety-three years. I know he's your uncle, but truth is truth, even if he is a fancy, big-time state senator. Believe me, if there's something shady going on or money to be made, you can bet that Philip Delacroix is involved some way. But what bothers me is where we're finding those stakes—too close to home for comfort.''

Remy reached out and took the old woman's bony hand. It was a hand that was callused from work, yet fragile with age. ''I don't want you worrying. I'm not going to let anything happen to your house.''

But Remy knew that what concerned Desiree was much more than just a matter of the small shack she called home. The old woman lived off the swamp. It not only supplied her with most of the food she ate, but also provided her with the many herbs she used in her medicines, and the raw ingredients for the crafts she sold to tourists. Any human disturbance in the delicate balance of nature could destroy her whole way of life.

''I'll get to the bottom of this thing, one way or another,'' he assured her.

Desiree smiled down at him, and Remy thought he detected something akin to pride shining in her faded eyes. ''I know you will,'' she said, squeezing his hand with surprising strength. ''As long as I've got you looking out for me, I don't worry, not really.'' She released his hand and backed toward the door. ''But for now, this old woman is tired and needs her rest, so I think I'll borrow your spare bedroom for a while. If your woman stirs or starts to run a fever, you come wake me, eh, *cher ami?*''

''Sure thing, *chère amie*,'' he answered, repeating the same Cajun endearment she had used.

After Desiree disappeared through the doorway, Remy yawned. Until his old friend had mentioned being tired, he hadn't realized just how exhausted he felt. He'd been up since before dawn and had spent most of the day searching for more signs of the poacher and more of the mysterious survey stakes.

Remy yawned again, and for a moment he was tempted to simply lie down beside the injured woman. Instead, he eased off of the bed and settled in the only chair in the room—a handmade wooden rocker with a woven cane seat, an antique he'd found stored in the attic of his family's home.

It was going to be a long night, he decided, leaning back and allowing himself the luxury of closing his eyes for a moment. But he'd had long nights before on stakeouts, and though it had been several years, the tricks of the trade on staying alert came back to him. Just like riding a bicycle—once learned, never forgotten.

DAWN WAS BREAKING over the trees, bathing the shadowy swamp with its pale pink hues, when Remy made his way to the kitchen the following morning.

As soon as he'd brewed a pot of coffee, he poured himself a cup. His patient was still unconscious and hadn't so much as groaned during the night.

He was staring out of the window above the sink when a bloodcurdling scream rent the air.

The woman!

Sudden adrenaline shot through his veins. The coffee mug slipped from his grasp and shattered in the sink. His heart thundering in his chest, Remy bolted for the bedroom.

# CHAPTER TWO

THE MOMENT SHE AWAKENED, she knew that something was wrong, terribly wrong. The reality of exactly what was wrong struck her like a venomous snake, and even as the scream died on her lips, paralyzing terror still streaked through her veins.

The pain... Oh, God, the pain. All feeling, all thought centered on the dull throbbing in her head and her arm. Instinctively she realized she should not make any sudden moves.

She tried to open her eyes, but the pain in her head escalated. God, it would be so much easier to simply sink back into the blessed oblivion of sleep. Surely this was a dream, she thought as desperation clawed at her insides, escaping in a groan. Surely this was a horrible nightmare. Any second now she would awaken, and the pain and confusion would be gone.

All she had to do was open her eyes.

The sound of heavy footsteps suddenly registered. Someone was running. Was this part of the dream?

She had to open her eyes!

And when she finally managed it, the sight of a strange man looming in the doorway nearly brought on another scream.

The man was tall, with a rawboned, sinewy look about him. His sandy hair was sprinkled with gray and had a shaggy, rumpled look about it. But it was the expression on his face that had her heart pumping overtime.

*If looks could kill.*

Oh, God. This wasn't a dream. This was real.

"Who—who are you?" she croaked.

With the swiftness of lightning, the harsh expression on his face gentled. "My name is Remy Delacroix," he said softly.

"Wh-where am I?"

He approached slowly, almost warily. "I found you injured and unconscious on Willow Island yesterday," he answered. "You have a gash on your head and a broken arm. It was almost dark—too late to take you to a hospital, so I brought you to my houseboat, instead."

"Houseboat? Willow Island? I—I..." Her lower lip quivered uncontrollably, and she covered her eyes with her left hand. "What's wrong with me?" She felt tears slide down her cheeks. "I—I can't seem to remember anything!"

"I'm sure it will all come back. Just give it time. Meanwhile, why don't we start with your name?"

She moaned, curling her hand into a tight fist. "You don't understand!" Behind the fist, she squeezed her eyes tightly shut. "I can't *remember* who I am. I can't *remember* my name."

For long moments there was nothing but silence in the room.

"It seems that the blow she got on her head did more than knock her unconscious."

At the unexpected sound of a woman's voice, she

opened her eyes. "Who is that?" she asked, searching the room. "Who else is here?"

The man stepped sideways, and an old woman appeared from behind him. "A friend," he answered. "Her name is Desiree, and she helped me take care of you last night."

Long strands of beads hung around the old woman's skinny neck. Huge gold hoops dangled from her earlobes, and a scarf held back abundant, wavy gray hair from a face full of wrinkles. Her expression was kind, however, and her eyes alert.

"Are you saying she has amnesia?" the man was asking.

"It appears so," the old woman answered, "but it's best to let a doctor look her over now to be sure."

The man...the old woman...amnesia... Suddenly, she was finding it hard to breathe. She gasped.

The man eased down beside the bed. "I know you're scared," he said gently. "But no one is going to hurt you." She wasn't sure if it was the tone of his voice or the sympathetic look on his face, but the panicky feeling began to subside somewhat.

"All we want to do is help you," he continued. "So if you think you're up to it, I'd like to take you to the clinic in town. It's a pretty competent facility, but the only way to get there is by boat, and the ride in will probably be uncomfortable for you."

"Town?"

"Bayou Beltane...Louisiana."

"But what happened to me? Was I in an accident?"

"I'm not quite sure exactly what happened yet," he answered. "I hoped that you could tell me." He paused, as if trying to decide what to say next. "I'm sorry," he finally said. "But I didn't find any identification on you, either."

The panicky feeling returned with a vengeance. No ID...a broken arm...a gash on her head...amnesia...

Threatening tears stung her eyes, and she blinked several times. Her stomach began to churn, as if she'd ingested something vile that was determined to rise up and choke her.

Who was she? she wondered frantically. What was her name? Did she have a family? A husband? Children? It was too much to think about, too confusing, and each time she tried to remember, her head felt as if it might explode.

If only her stomach would settle down, her arm stop aching and her head stop throbbing, she might be able to concentrate. But for now, she seemed to have no choice except to trust this man who called himself Remy...and the old lady—what had he called her? Desiree?

An odd name, she thought. Exotic. But it seemed to fit the old woman. Desperate to focus on anything but her frightening situation, she stared at her.

There was something hypnotic and unnerving about the older woman's eyes, and for a moment she fancied that Desiree could see clear to the depths of her soul. Her instinct was to look away, to break the contact, but she couldn't seem to do so.

Then suddenly, bits of memory flashed in and out of her mind. The flashes were too disjointed and fleeting to grasp, and the effort of trying to capture them made her head hurt worse.

"I guess this sounds strange," she murmured, still

staring at Desiree, "especially since I can't even remember my own name, but I feel as if I should know
you. Have we met before?"

For a second, something akin to surprised satisfaction flickered over Desiree's face. But the moment
passed all too soon. "We've never met," the old
woman said.

And as Desiree slowly shook her head, denying
any acquaintance, it was as if the old woman had
released her mesmerizing hold. The young woman
was finally able to break eye contact and look away.

"Desiree took care of you last night," Remy explained. "Maybe that's why you think you know
her."

"Maybe so," she murmured, lowering her gaze to
the white sheet that covered her. But she didn't think
so, especially since the man had taken care of her,
too, and she didn't have the same odd sense of recognition with him.

She glanced up at him, and unlike when she'd
gazed into Desiree's eyes and wanted to look away,
his eyes invited and held her attention. Deep set and
framed by prominent brows that were a shade darker
than his hair, they were a piercing emerald green.
She could well imagine those eyes being able to quell
a person with a single look, yet there was a direct
honesty in them also, the kind that inspired trust.

Trust...did she trust him? Once more she felt blind
panic well up within her, and for a second, she feared
she would begin screaming again.

As if he knew what she was feeling, Remy reached
out and squeezed her hand. "Don't be scared," he
whispered. "It's going to be okay."

She couldn't explain it, but something about his soft words along with his warm, comforting touch seemed to have the power to chase away the panic.

She could trust him, she decided. She had no choice. For now.

"Are you hungry?" Remy released her hand, and strangely, she found herself wanting to hold on. "I can fix you something—"

"No food," Desiree interrupted. "Maybe a cup of tea, but I don't think it's wise for her to eat anything before a doctor sees her."

"I don't think I could keep anything solid down just yet, anyway," she whispered as she tucked her hand beneath the sheet. "But I—I am thirsty."

"I'll get the tea while Remy helps you sit up. Then you probably need to visit the bathroom before the boat trip to the clinic." Desiree shot Remy a warning look. "Slowly. No sudden moves."

The next half hour passed in a blur of pain, bouts of dizziness that threatened to render her unconscious again and acute embarrassment for being so helpless and dependent on the man named Remy.

By the time Remy carried her to the boat for the trip to town, she was having a hard time holding back tears of frustration and self-consciousness. The least bit of movement made her dizzy, and she found herself clinging to him. It was only his no-nonsense attitude and extreme gentleness that made the whole ordeal bearable at all.

ONCE AGAIN REMY used life jackets and the spare blanket to fix a makeshift bed in the bottom of his boat, but this time he added a couple of pillows to cushion his passenger's ride.

When he finally eased the craft away from the dock, the sun was peeping over the treetops, burning off the last of the mist. Once he'd maneuvered to the middle of the bayou, he geared down the motor to a slow and easy speed in hopes of sparing the woman any more discomfort than she'd already experienced.

It was a beautiful, cloudless day, early enough so that the cool of the night still lingered over the murky, quiet waters, and the steady breeze from the movement of the boat carried the potent, earthy fragrance of the swamp. From time to time they startled a small flock of wood ducks as they passed, or a great blue heron fishing in the shallows. Remy watched his passenger staring at the passing scenery. He could tell that the past half hour had taken a toll, both physical and mental, so by an unspoken, mutual agreement, the first few minutes of the boat ride down the bayou were silent ones.

She was the first to break the silence. "It's so beautiful out here," she said over the low drone of the motor as she glanced up at him. Then, like a dark cloud racing across the sun, a shadow passed over her eyes, and she slowly returned her gaze to the passing trees. "I only wish I could remember why I came here in the first place," she murmured.

Whether it was her tone or the lost, haunted look on her face, Remy wasn't sure, but suddenly something sharp and painful twisted inside him. It was at that moment that he finally realized what had been happening to him, why he'd felt so strange since the first moment he'd discovered the injured woman.

Some of the old feelings that he'd thought had shriveled up and died when he'd buried Julie—feelings like compassion, tenderness, sympathy—were stirring to life again. And oddly enough, all because of this particular woman.

*But why now?* he wondered. *Why with this perfect stranger?* Remy didn't have an answer, at least not one that made sense.

Unsettled to the point that sensible conversation was impossible, he was relieved that the woman seemed content with silence for the remainder of the trip down the bayou.

By the time he sighted the landing for the Willow Island Swamp Tours headquarters and gift shop, where he kept his truck parked, Remy was once again feeling more in control and had decided that his reaction to the woman was a simple matter of too many hours without sleep.

Since it was way too early for the shop to open, no one was around when he pulled alongside the pier. Though he was relieved that he wouldn't have to waste time explaining his passenger to his curious employees, he made a mental note to check the boat-rental logbook the first opportunity he got. There was a good chance that his mystery lady had rented the boat he'd found drifting, and if so, her name would be listed there.

As Remy tied up his craft, without warning, the woman tried to stand.

"Hey, wait a minute," he called, but before he could get to her, she paled and sank back onto the life jackets with a groan.

Remy stepped back into the boat and knelt down

beside her. "What the hell did you think you were doing? Another stunt like that and I'll have to fish you out of the bayou."

"Sorry," she whispered. "But could you please stop shouting at me? It makes my head hurt. I thought I might be able to walk, but I'm too dizzy. I just hate being so damn helpless."

Remy took a deep breath and let it out with a sigh. Feeling helpless was something he understood all too well. "I'm the one who should apologize," he said gruffly. "I overreacted. But there's no use in taking foolish chances, so why don't you save us both a lot of trouble and resign yourself to the fact that I'm going to be carrying you until I get you to the clinic?"

She didn't reply, but she didn't have to say anything. Her exasperated expression said it all.

BAYOU BELTANE MEDICAL Clinic, a short, five-minute drive away, was a small, privately owned, twenty-bed hospital that supported two ambulances. Its small emergency room was equipped for minor surgeries, and most of the time it was adequate for the small community's everyday needs. For more serious cases, patients were transported to either Northern Hospital or Slidell Memorial.

"No sudden movements now," Remy reminded the woman as he parked the truck and switched off the engine.

When she cut him a glance that could have frozen swamp water, he almost grinned. Neither of them knew her name, but one thing he did know was that the lady showed definite signs of being independent, a woman used to doing for herself.

The waiting room in the clinic was empty when Remy entered, the injured woman in his arms. After he'd eased her down on the nearest sofa, he walked over and spoke to the receptionist.

A minute later, a nurse he'd never seen before appeared pushing a wheelchair.

Once the nurse had settled the patient on a narrow examination table in a curtained cubicle, she tried to oust Remy. "Mr. Delacroix, you have to wait outside."

Remy glanced at his charge, and for all her independence, and though she tried valiantly to hide it, he could tell she was terrified. Hell, who wouldn't be in her situation? he thought.

"I'll stay," he said firmly, thinking that she might feel less fearful if she could see a familiar face.

The nurse shook her head. "I'm sorry, but you can't. I need to undress her, and the doctor will want to examine her. Since you're not a relative—"

"So I'll turn my back."

"You have to leave, sir."

"I'm not leaving her, so you can just forget it!"

"Come on, Remy," a gruff voice called out from the other side of the curtain. "Nora is new here—just moved to town from Mobile. Good nurses are hard to come by, so be nice and do what she says."

Instantly recognizing the voice of an old friend, Dr. Sam White, Remy relaxed. He felt a bit more at ease knowing that Sam was on duty and would be tending to the injured woman. Sam was one of two general practitioners who ran the clinic, and Remy and Sam went back a long way—back to high school days, when the two of them had been rivals for the quarterback position on the football team. Finding them equally talented, the coach had finally decided to use them both, alternating them each game, and the two had remained fast friends ever since.

Remy reached out and squeezed the injured woman's shoulder. "The doctor who's going to examine you is an old friend and he'll take good care of you. I won't be far if you need me."

Then, with a shrug and an apologetic glance at the nurse, Remy left the cubicle.

An hour passed before Sam sought out Remy. After shaking hands and clapping him on the back, the doctor tried to cover a yawn. "I've been up most of the night waiting for Bayou Beltane's newest citizen to arrive—a fine baby boy, I might add—so could we talk over a cup of coffee?"

When Remy hesitated, Sam nudged him toward the doorway leading to the small room that served as a makeshift cafeteria. "She's doing fine. A nurse is getting her settled into a room, and then you'll be able to see her."

Remy trusted Sam and had learned a long time ago that his friend couldn't be rushed. It was a trait that had made Sam such a good quarterback as well as a fine doctor, so with a shrug, he gave in and followed him.

Once they were seated, Sam took a long drink of his coffee, then gave Remy his full attention. "Before I get started, be sure and tell Desiree that, as usual, she did a great job. I couldn't have set that arm better, but—" he chuckled and amusement danced in his eyes ''—you can also tell her that if she doesn't stop practicing medicine without a license, I'm going to file charges.''

Remy grinned, knowing that Sam's threat was empty. Like Remy, Sam had known Desiree most of his life, and he loved to irritate her. And of course, Desiree usually gave back as good as she got by completely ignoring him.

Sam shook his head. ''That old woman should have been a doctor,'' he muttered, then cleared his throat. ''Now...about our patient. As you're already aware, the lady has amnesia. Most probably the post-traumatic retrograde type, since it's obvious she received a head trauma. She also has a slight concussion and a fractured elbow, so I'm keeping her in the clinic for a couple of days. Just a precaution,'' he added.

''How long will the amnesia last?''

Sam shrugged. ''There's no way to know for sure. Could be a day or two. Could be longer, but like I told our mystery lady, this particular type is never permanent.'' He paused to take another sip of his coffee. ''I thought she was one of your tourists, but she says that you found her on Willow Island, so why don't you fill me in?''

For a moment, Remy hesitated. He'd known Sam long enough to recognize when his friend was fishing for information. And while it was true that he trusted Sam, it was also true that if foul play was suspected, Sam would be obligated under law to report it, and that was something Remy didn't want. Not yet.

Making a quick decision to leave out his suspicions as well as his speculations, Remy explained how he'd found the woman, giving the impression that she'd simply had an accident.

When he'd finished, Sam had a thoughtful frown on his face. "Anything is possible, I suppose, but I'm finding it hard to believe that the blow she received to her head was an accident." He raised an eyebrow. "Is there something you're not telling me?"

His eyes never wavering, Remy slowly shook his head. "There's nothing to tell...right now. If and when there is, you'll be the first to know."

"Have you reported this to Jake yet?"

"I haven't had time," Remy hedged.

For long moments Sam continued staring at Remy, his gaze steady and probing. Then, as if satisfied at what he saw, he finally glanced away. "Be sure you do," he said gruffly. "Like I told you, I'm going to keep her here for a couple of days, but after that, unless we find out who she is, a report needs to filed with Jake. My guess is that he will either place her in sheltered accommodation or put her up in a motel. My bet would be the shelter, since the staff who run it are good people and could keep an eye on her."

Remy had given the situation a lot of thought while cooling his heels in the waiting room. What he needed was to buy some time, time in which he could track down her identity and that of the person who'd attacked her. It had been awhile since Remy had felt so strongly about anything, but whoever had done this had made the mistake of doing it on Willow Island, in a part of the swamp that Remy considered his personal turf. And in his swamp, Remy Delacroix meted out justice.

Sam leaned back in the chair. "Either I can file an official report or you can. It will be your choice."

Remy understood that his friend was giving him a warning. Sam would give him the time he needed, no questions asked. But he would only go so far.

Remy nodded, indicating that he understood exactly what Sam was saying. "I'll do it," he said. *Just not right away,* he added silently.

Whoever had tried to kill her might try again. For the time being, it would be safer for her if the attacker thought he'd succeeded, and Remy figured that the fewer people who knew about her, the better, including the sheriff.

Now all he had to do was figure out a way to tell the woman what he suspected.

# CHAPTER THREE

WHEN REMY ENTERED the small hospital room an hour later, his mystery lady was asleep. Lying against the white pillow and dressed in a pastel hospital gown, she looked helpless and vulnerable. A plaster cast from elbow to wrist had replaced the makeshift splint, and a different bandage covered her head wound.

Satisfied that she was okay for the moment, he slipped back out of the room, and after glancing at his watch and noting the time, he searched for a pay phone.

He found one hiding in a corner of the hallway outside the clinic waiting room. The first call he placed was to his gift shop. One of the guides, a young man named Ray, answered.

"Ray, I need to speak to Claudia."

"Sorry, boss, but she hasn't shown up yet."

Remy frowned, wondering what was going on. Claudia was one of the most dependable employees he had. She was a part-time student who, along with helping out in the gift shop, took reservations for the tours, sold fishing tackle and bait, and rented out boats. In the three years she had worked for him, she'd never been late, not without calling in first.

"I'm sure she'll show up soon," Remy said,

speaking his thoughts out loud and silently cursing the fact that Claudia had never bothered to have a phone installed in the tiny houseboat she rented. "In the meantime, maybe you can help me out here," he said. "I need some information from the boat-rental logbook. It should be somewhere near the cash register."

Several moments passed without a response from Ray. "I'm looking," he finally said, "but I don't see it. Maybe it's locked up in the office."

"Damn," Remy muttered. Besides his own, Claudia had the only other office key.

"Thanks, anyway, Ray. I'll check back later." Remy had almost hung up the phone when something else suddenly occurred to him. "Hey, Ray, hold on a second!"

He could have kicked himself for not thinking of it before. If his mystery lady *was* the person who had rented the boat he'd found, and assuming that she hadn't walked or arrived with a tour group or on one of the hotel shuttle buses, then she would have left her car in the gift shop parking lot. He could have a check run on her license plate and find out her identity that way. It was a long shot, but one worth checking out.

"Remy? You wanted something else?"

Ray's voice shook him out of his reverie. "Did you notice a car in the guest parking lot when you came to work?"

For a second, the line was silent. "Uh, boss, I—I was kinda late myself this morning, so when I got here, the lot was full and there were people waiting."

Remy grimaced. Unlike Claudia, this wasn't the

first time that Ray had been late for work, and Remy made a mental note to have a long, frank discussion with him. But for now, all he could do was wait until the end of the day to see if a car was left in the parking lot.

"Okay, never mind for now, but there's one more thing I need you to do for me. One of the rental boats is stranded on Willow Island—beached on the north shore. Get someone to take you out there and bring the boat in."

Without waiting for an answer or giving an explanation, Remy hung up the phone and stared thoughtfully at the gray tiled floor. Again he had to ask himself how he'd missed such an obvious clue as the woman's car. But he didn't like the answer he came up with.

His mystery lady was consuming his thoughts, to the point of distraction. Never mind that it had been four years since he'd worked as a detective; he'd been trained to be observant. And never mind that, unlike the employees' parking area behind the building, the customers' lot was screened by a stand of trees. There was only one explanation for his obvious oversight. The woman was having a strange effect on him, making him lose all objectivity, stirring up emotions he hadn't felt in years....

Remy closed his eyes for a moment and tried to clear his head. *Think, man. Concentrate. Do what you were trained to do. Her identity...hell, her life might depend on it.*

With a sigh, he fished his billfold out of his back pocket and riffled through it until he found the small card he was looking for. Within seconds, Remy had the New Orleans Police Academy on the line.

"Charly Delacroix, please."

Remy was put on hold. Bracing himself against the wall with his hand, he drummed an impatient staccato rhythm with his fingers while he waited. Though he'd broken all ties with the New Orleans Police Department when he'd resigned, he still had official connections through his niece, Charly, who attended the police academy by day and worked as an NOPD computer tech by night.

He hated the idea of his niece becoming a cop, but he was relieved that when she finished the academy, she wanted to work in Slidell instead of New Orleans. Otherwise he would have lived in fear that fallout from the hornet's nest he had stirred up in the NOPD before he'd resigned might have eventually filtered down to her.

Remy pushed himself away from the wall. It was too early for a missing person's report to have been filed yet, but he could at least alert his niece to be on the lookout for one involving a female in case any came through during the next couple of days.

With a thoughtful frown on his face Remy said goodbye to his niece and hung up the phone then walked slowly back toward the room where the injured woman lay sleeping. If he had to, he could have Charly run a fingerprint check on her. It was a long shot at best, since there was no reason an average person would have fingerprints on file, and he doubted it would turn up anything, but he still needed to cover all the bases. Determining her identity through the license plate on her car was still a possibility, but the only thing he could do now was wait.

Entering the hospital room, Remy walked to the bed and stared at the woman, who was still sleeping. Sam had told him she would probably sleep most of the afternoon, and there was always the chance that when she woke up this time, she might remember something.

Without thinking, Remy reached out his hand, intending to brush a strand of hair from her face. Just before he touched her, he jerked his hand back and closed it into a fist. With his insides churning, he abruptly turned away and walked purposely to the lounge chair in the corner of the room, all the time reminding himself that he had no right to take such liberties. She was a total stranger whom he knew absolutely nothing about. A woman who, for reasons unknown, someone had assaulted and left for dead. He would do well to keep his distance, physically and emotionally, despite the crazy emotions just being near her stirred up inside him.

*SHE WAS LOST, wandering in a fog so thick that it was hard to breathe. It swirled around her like an undulating, evil whirlwind, and with each step she took it seemed to grow more dense, until she couldn't see her hand when she held it out in front of her.*

*Then suddenly, the heavy mist parted, just enough to see that a bright light lay just beyond. If she could somehow escape the fog and get to the light, she knew she could find her way home. But mud pulled and sucked at her feet, and the faster she tried to run, the slower she seemed to move.*

*Then the light began to flicker and grow dimmer, and the gap in the fog began to close again. She opened her mouth to scream, but no sound came....*

She awoke with a start and her heart raced in her chest.

A nightmare, she thought. Just another terrible dream.

Then she remembered where she was and why, and she wondered which was worse—the sleeping nightmare or the one she'd awakened to.

Nothing had changed. She still didn't know who she was, still couldn't recall her own name. Staring up at the white ceiling, she blinked back tears and took deep, even breaths. Panicking and losing control wouldn't change things, wouldn't help her remember or regain what she'd lost.

Then it suddenly occurred to her that at least one thing *had* changed. The throbbing pain in her head had almost completely disappeared. Testing it out, she slowly turned her head, first to her left side and then to the right.

That was when she saw him. Remy Delacroix was stretched out on a recliner in the corner of the room, his hooded, bloodshot eyes watching her every move.

A shiver of unease raised gooseflesh on her arms. Just knowing that he'd been sitting there watching her while she slept made her feel funny, uneasy... self-conscious? Whichever, it was ridiculous, considering all that he'd done for her.

"How are you feeling?"

"B-better," she answered. "My head doesn't hurt as bad, and my arm..." She glanced down at the snow-white cast that enclosed her right arm and shrugged. "It aches, but it's bearable."

"What about your memory?" he prompted.

While the question was straightforward enough, and nothing about his appearance showed anything but polite concern, there was a cautious note in his voice that set off warning bells in her head.

"Unfortunately, nothing," she answered, still staring at the cast and wondering why she was suddenly having such suspicious thoughts about him. And why was he still hanging around? Whatever responsibility he'd felt for being the one who had found her had surely ended once he'd delivered her to the clinic. So why hadn't he left?

"That's too bad," he said.

The warning bells grew louder and she stared at him.

"I was really hoping you could shed some light on a few things...."

"What kind of things?"

He leaned forward and rested his elbows on the arms of the chair. "I have good reason to believe that your so-called accident wasn't an accident."

"I—I don't understand. What do you mean?"

"For one thing, even if you had slipped and fallen, there was nothing you could have hit your head on where I found you. And for another thing, the wound you have is more the type that comes from a blow with a blunt instrument."

"No!" she whispered, shaking her head.

He nodded slowly. "Unfortunately, it is."

"Are you saying that someone assaulted me, knocked me unconscious on—on purpose?"

He nodded again. "And I also believe they left you there, knowing that you would eventually die from exposure."

Chills of terror chased down her spine. "But why?" she cried. "Why would anyone want to hurt me?"

"That, along with your identity, is what I intend to find out."

All she could do was stare at him. But even as she tried to absorb the shock of what he'd just told her, other thoughts intruded. Dark, suspicious thoughts. Again she had to ask herself why he was still hanging around, why he hadn't left. What would make him so concerned about a perfect stranger, unless...

Was it possible? she wondered, even as every instinct within her wanted to deny the niggling suspicions. Could he be responsible for what had happened to her—responsible for her so-called "accident"? Was that the reason he was so interested in whether she had regained her memory, why he was still here?

She looked at him again, but all she saw was genuine, polite regard. No, she thought. Not once had he given her reason to distrust him or his motives. Just the opposite, in fact. So why was she harboring such thoughts? Suddenly ashamed of being so distrustful after all he'd done for her, she broke eye contact with him and focused on the wall in front of her.

"Sam assured me your memory would come back."

"He told me the same thing," she mumbled distractedly. Until her memory returned, she at least owed Remy the benefit of the doubt. Didn't she? Maybe if she knew more about him…

"What do you do?" she asked bluntly, shifting her gaze back toward him. But as soon as she asked the question, she realized how abrupt and rude it sounded, and she felt her cheeks grow warm with embarrassment. "I'm sorry. I don't mean to pry. I—I guess I'm just curious," she quickly explained. "Especially since you're the one who rescued me."

With a dismissive wave, he settled back in the chair. "Don't apologize. If I were in your place, I'd be curious, too. And just as scared," he added softly. "But to answer your question, I'm a tour guide and owner of Willow Island Swamp Tours."

"Why a swamp-tour guide—I mean, how did you get into something like that?"

Remy sighed. His family kept asking the same questions. But unlike with them, Remy didn't sense disapproval in the woman's tone or expression—only genuine curiosity. Since keeping her talking seemed to be the best way of taking her mind off her own situation, he decided to give her an answer instead of ignoring her the way he'd learned to do with his family.

He shrugged. "I got tired of the rat race and decided to move back to Bayou Beltane. I grew up in this area, and you might say the swamp was my home away from home when I was a boy. The old man who ran Willow Island Swamp Tours wanted to retire, so I bought him out."

His explanation for moving back home didn't begin to describe what he'd felt four years ago, and for an uneasy moment, all the old bitterness, anger and disillusionment he'd experienced during that troubled time threatened to surface. It was one of the reasons he never talked about his past.

Remy took a deep breath. That was then and this was now, he reminded himself. "Tourists are fascinated by the swamps here in Louisiana," he continued. "They come to see the gators, and also the deer, the coons, the muskrats—sometimes we even catch sight of a bobcat. Along with the tours, I run a gift shop, sell fishing tackle and bait, and rent out boats."

For a moment, he was tempted to tell her that it was because of one of his rental boats that he'd found her in the first place, and that he might soon be able to provide her with her name. But instinct cautioned him against getting her hopes up, and the moment passed.

"All of that must keep you pretty busy."

"I do stay busy," he agreed. "But I also have several good, competent employees who help me."

Remy could tell she was impressed, but impressing her hadn't been his intention, and he'd only meant his monologue as a diversion. Still, it was nice for a change to have someone genuinely interested. He only wished his family could see past their bias to understand his love of the outdoors, or at least quit bugging him about his current occupation. It wasn't even a matter of wanting their approval. Remy had always been a bit of a black sheep, anyway, not quite living up to the wealthy Delacroix standards. But the family gatherings he had to attend were always slightly awkward, and being around his socially prominent relatives, especially his father and brother, was like walking through a mine field of emotion.

"That woman—Desiree—tell me about her."

The change of subject was a welcome relief from his dark thoughts, and a grin pulled at Remy's lips. "I've known Desiree all my life. She worked for my grandparents when she was a girl, and we're very old, very good friends...and business associates. Desiree keeps my gift shop supplied with local crafts and various concoctions of tea, herbs and spices that she makes from ingredients she gathers from the swamp."

"How is she able to do all that? She must be at least eighty."

This time Remy grinned widely. "Not quite eighty. More like ninety-three?"

"No way." The woman shook her head and winced.

It was obvious that the sudden movement had caused her pain, but to her credit, she didn't give in to it or complain, and after only a brief moment of hesitation, she continued. "I knew there was something about her. Something unusual, but—"

"Desiree *is* unusual, in every respect. And unique," Remy added. "She's a healer. Some call them white witches. But she's also a quadroon and very proud of her heritage."

The woman shook her head as if puzzled.

"A quadroon is the result of racially mixed parentage," he explained. "One-fourth black and three-fourths white."

"I know the definition of quadroon," she said evenly, "but I still can't believe she's ninety-three."

"I can assure you she is, but I know what you mean. Even for me, it's sometimes hard to believe."

For a moment, the woman continued staring at him. "Yes...hard to believe," she repeated softly. "But right now I'm finding everything hard to believe."

It was there again—that lost, haunted look in her eyes, and Remy shifted uneasily in the chair. If only there was something he could say or do to reassure her, to erase that look.

"Are you hungry?" he finally asked, hoping to at least distract her again. "Can I get you something to eat?"

"No...maybe later," she murmured. Then, with a hopeless sigh, she closed her eyes and turned away from him. "If you don't mind, I'm still tired," she said, curling up into a fetal position beneath the sheet. "I think I'll just sleep for now."

The sight of her small, huddled form beneath the sheet hit him like a physical blow, and an acute sensation of helplessness washed over him. There had to be something he could do to help her *now*, some way to give her back her identity. But what?

Seized with a sudden restless urgency, Remy glanced at his watch. His best bet was the logbook. Surely by now, Claudia had shown up or had at least called in.

He stood. "I need to make a phone call," he said quietly. "But I'll be back to check on you."

He knew the woman was probably still awake, and for a moment he waited, hoping for a response of some kind. When she didn't offer one, he decided to go make his call. Hopefully when he returned, he

would have some good news for her—at least a
name, if nothing else. Anything to take away that
look he'd seen in her dark eyes.

## CHAPTER FOUR

WHEN THE PHONE RANG in the gift shop, Claudia
Landry glared at it, then forced a smile as she rang
up her next customer's purchase. It was bad enough
that she'd been late for work, thanks to a dead battery
in her old clunker of a car, but the minute she'd
arrived, Ray had taken off like a shot, mumbling
something about getting a phone call from the boss
and needing to check on one of the rental boats for
him.

And now the incessant ringing of the phone, along
with the group of tourists throwing questions at her
about the delay of the tour that Ray was scheduled
to take out, was enough to make her want to throw
up her hands and walk out. And just where was
Remy this morning? Claudia wondered impatiently,
leaning across the counter to snag the phone receiver.

"Willow Island Swamp Tours," she intoned, unable to disguise the irritation she felt.

"Where have you been?"

Recognizing Remy's voice, Claudia closed her
eyes and counted to ten. *Ask and ye shall receive,*
she thought, recalling one of her childhood Sunday
school verses.

"I'm sorry I was late," she said, "but it's a long

story and I'm up to my eyeballs with customers. Where the heck are you?''

''It's a long story,'' Remy teasingly drawled, repeating her own words. ''But I won't be in today or tomorrow, and it sounds like you're pretty busy.''

''You don't know the half of it. Ray was supposed to take out the nine o'clock tour, but he raced off—said he had an errand to run. He's gonna throw the whole schedule off, and there's people everywhere—''

''Whoa! Calm down, Claudia. None of the tourists are going anywhere until Ray gets back. I asked him to retrieve an abandoned rental boat I found yesterday. That's one of the reasons I called.''

Claudia was staring at a growing line of people waiting to check out gift-shop purchases. Then, like an instant replay, it suddenly hit her what he'd just said. ''What abandoned boat? There ain't no missing boats. All of them was returned…at least I *think* they was. I had to leave Ray in charge yesterday afternoon 'cause I had an appointment, so I can't say for sure. Maybe I forgot to tell him to check the rentals at the end of the day.''

''One of them didn't return,'' Remy said evenly.

''Oh, great!'' She blew her bangs out of her eyes. ''Look, Remy, this ain't no excuse, but Ray wouldn't a knowed he was supposed to check the rentals unless I told him to. The guides never have to do that kind of stuff.''

''Never mind that now. Do you remember renting out one of our boats to a woman? Blond with brown eyes, about five foot six or seven, wearing khaki shorts and a white cotton blouse?''

"Yeah, that rings a bell," Claudia answered.

"Do you happen to recall if she gave a name?" Remy could hear the background noise of the shop—tourists talking and laughing—but it was several moments before Claudia answered.

"I…honestly, boss I don't remember, b-but things were a bit hectic at the time." Being a milder, somewhat cooler month for south Louisiana, November was always a busy time for the swamp-tour business. "I had to leave early 'cause I had that appointment at school," she continued, "You know, to figure out my next course. Anyways, I was trying to do up everything so I could go. And, uh, Joey showed up and I—I…he was…"

"Drunk," Remy finished for her. "And causing another one of his famous scenes, no doubt."

"I'm sorry, Remy. I tried to get rid of him, but you know how he gets."

When Joey showed up drunk, Remy could well imagine Claudia being so humiliated that she wouldn't be able to recall a customer's name even if she'd spelled it twice, or anything else, for that matter. Claudia's brothers had succeeded in causing such a ruckus at her previous two jobs that she'd been fired. Remy strongly suspected that they'd done so on purpose, in an attempt to force their sister to move back home.

"It's okay, hon," he said evenly. "It's not your fault." The one thing she didn't need from him was more grief. Having lost her mother when she was a child, she'd had enough hassles dealt out to her from her father and four lazy brothers to last her a lifetime. As far as Remy was concerned, they were all a bunch of ignorant, good-for-nothing bums whose sole purpose in life was to try to make Claudia feel guilty for having moved out, leaving them to fend for themselves.

With a sigh, he pinched the bridge of his nose. "Okay, Claudia," he said, trying to rein in his impatience. "What I need from you are the names off the logbook of everyone who rented boats yesterday."

"Oh, sure. Just a second."

Remy sighed when several minutes passed without a response. "Claudia?"

"Uh…yeah, sure. I'm looking, I'm looking."

"Try looking in the office," he suggested evenly.

CLAUDIA FINALLY LOCATED the logbook on the desk in Remy's office. Snatching it up, she rushed back out to the counter. Zeroing in on the growing line of customers, she didn't see the fair-haired man headed her way until it was too late.

The collision almost knocked the breath out of her, and she would have fallen flat on her butt if he hadn't grabbed her arms to steady her.

"Oh, I'm so sorry…" When she looked up and saw who she'd collided with, the breath left her body for the second time in the space of mere seconds. Of all the people in the world—of all the *men* in the world—the last person she wanted to appear like a klutz in front of was Bernard Leroux.

"Hey, pip-squeak." A gravelly chuckle rumbled in his broad chest. "You better slow down and watch where you're going, eh, *chere?*"

A funny feeling fluttered in her tummy, and her

arms tingled where his large hands held her. "D-don't c-call me pip-squeak," she stammered self-consciously as she jerked away and backed toward the counter.

Mortification followed by a telltale burning in her cheeks made Claudia want to sink into the floor. Instead, she snatched up the phone receiver, then turned her back to Bernard and the wide-eyed tourists.

The first time she had seen Bernard Leroux standing on the deck of his charter boat, he'd been dressed in a pair of cutoff jeans and nothing else. Having grown up with four older brothers, she'd seen half-dressed men before. But looking at Bernard was different. The moment he'd docked his boat at the Willow Island Swamp Tours pier, she'd experienced exactly what love at first sight meant.

That particular incident had taken place six months ago, and each time she'd seen him since, not only did she find some way to make a complete fool out of herself by knocking something over or stumbling—usually over her own feet—but the feelings she'd experienced that first day had intensified tenfold.

Claudia was a realist, however; a man like Bernard would never be attracted to a woman like her. He'd want someone beautiful, someone sophisticated, so she tried her best to hide her feelings anytime she was around him. It was bad enough to experience unrequited love without the humiliation of him finding out how she felt about him.

Claudia cleared her throat and tried to ignore the

fact that Bernard was wandering around in the gift shop. "Remy, I found the logbook."

"Well, read me the names," he instructed, his tone bordering on impatient.

The closest she could recall, there had been only five or six rentals the day before. Claudia flipped through the pages until she found the right place. "Hmm...okay, I got her right here." She read off the list, but hesitated when she saw the last entry.

"Is that all?" Remy asked.

"Them's all the names. The last one's got to be a company of some sort—uh, Environmental Standards—and it lists a Baton Rouge post office box for an address."

"Environmental Standards..." Remy repeated, as if thinking aloud. "I think there's a state government agency called the Department of Environmental Standards. Is there a phone number given?"

"Yeah, and there's some initials. But Remy, when you gonna tell me what's going on? Is the missing boat the one the woman rented?"

"Initials? What initials?"

"You know, like in initials a name."

"What are they?"

"The handwriting's kind of scrawled, but it looks like a *J*, a *K* and a *D*. So, boss, what's this all about?"

"Are you sure about the initials?" Remy pressed.

"Pretty sure. Like I said, they're kind of scrawly...uh-oh!" Claudia swallowed hard. "I just remembered—the woman did flash an ID card at me, but all I looked at was the picture. You know, to make sure it matched her face. But then Joey started causing a ruckus, so I didn't get a chance to look for her name. Remy, I'm sorry, I—"

"It's okay, hon. Stop apologizing. I understand. So how about that telephone number?"

"Sure," she answered with a sigh of relief. Remy Delacroix was, at times, a hard man, but no one could ever accuse him of being unfair, and Claudia felt fortunate indeed to have him for a boss as well as a friend. "Okay, here goes. The number is—"

"Wait a second. I don't have a pen handy. Hold on while I get one."

"Remy, I got a slew of customers waiting!" But it was already too late. There was nothing but silence on the line. Either he hadn't heard her or he'd ignored her.

With a grimace of impatience, she wedged the receiver between her shoulder and chin, faced the waiting customers and began ringing up the purchases of the first tourist.

She waited on two more tourists before Remy finally spoke in her ear. "Okay, give me the number."

Claudia held up her hand and forced a smile for the next customer. "Just a minute, please," she mouthed. Then she turned back to where she'd placed the logbook and read off the phone number to Remy.

"Thanks," Remy said. "Just one more thing," he added. "After closing today, I want you to check the customer parking lot. If there's a car left, take down the license plate number for me. I'll call back for it later this evening."

Curiosity burned within Claudia, and she was

tempted to press the issue and question him further. But knowing Remy as she did, she knew he wouldn't tell her anything until he was good and ready. And besides, customers were waiting.

REMY DEPRESSED the hook, and when he heard a dial tone, he placed a call, using the number Claudia had given him.

He tensed when the call went through and began ringing. This could be the break he was looking for, he thought as he waited for someone to answer. If, as he suspected, "Environmental Standards" was in fact the Louisiana Department of Environmental Standards, then there was a good possibility that his mystery lady worked for them. And with the initials, it shouldn't be too hard to track down her name. It also meant that there was a good possibility she had some connection with the survey stakes he'd been finding.

"Louisiana Department of Environmental Standards. How may I help you?"

*Bingo!* "Hello, I'm calling to inquire about one of your employees. She's—"

"I'm sorry, sir, but we're not allowed to give out information about employees."

"This is a very important matter. Is there someone else I can talk to—a supervisor or the head of the department?"

There was a pause on the other end of the line. "Well," the woman finally answered, "I guess you could talk with Mr. Talbot, but he isn't in today."

"Anyone else?"

"No, sir. Mr. Talbot is the department head and the only one who would be able to help you."

"When will he be in?" Remy asked evenly, a sinking feeling settling in his gut.

"Um, today is Tuesday, Thursday is Thanksgiving, and since we're closed Thursday and Friday for the holiday, and he has the flu, I suspect he won't be back in until next Monday."

"Is there another number where I can reach him?"

"I'm sorry, but no. His home phone number is unlisted."

For a moment Remy wondered if it would do any good to push the matter further. Probably not, he finally decided. After all, the receptionist was simply doing her job. "Thanks, anyway," he finally said, unable to disguise the disappointment he felt. Then he carefully hung up the receiver.

For several minutes, he stood staring at the phone. He still had his ace in the hole, he told himself. If his mystery woman had left a car in the parking lot, he could trace her through the license plate.

His mind raced with possibilities. Willow Island Swamp Tours was only a five-minute drive from the clinic, and for a moment he was tempted to leap in his truck and check out the parking lot himself. If he copied down all the license-plate numbers in the parking lot...

*And what good would that do?* a voice of reason and logic asked.

Punch-drunk, he decided. He was so punch-drunk from lack of sleep and so frustrated with his inability to find out anything that he was beginning to grasp at straws. It made more sense to check out the cars left after closing, so there was nothing to be done at the moment but wait. With a grimace, he walked away from the phone and headed back down the hallway in the direction of the mystery lady's room.

"Remy?"

At the sound of Desiree's voice, Remy stopped and turned, waiting until she caught up with him.

"How is your woman?" she asked softly.

Remy shrugged. "She says better. Her head doesn't hurt as much as before, but…"

"But no memory yet."

He nodded.

"What does that young upstart Samuel say about it?"

In spite of his surly mood, Remy felt a grin tugging at his lips. Desiree always insisted on using Sam's full name, something that irritated the doctor to no end, since he'd never liked the name Samuel, anyway. "About what you suspect, I imagine. That it will return eventually."

Desiree reached out and patted Remy's upper arm. "You should probably stay with her until it does…just in case. She needs someone to watch over her, to protect her in case that *couillon* who did this decides to finish what he started."

Remy reached up and rubbed the back of his neck. "Yeah, I've been thinking about that. I think the fewer people who know about her, the better. At least for now."

Desiree nodded in agreement. "And when Samuel says she can leave, you will take her home with you, *non?*"

Remy hesitated. "I hope it doesn't come to that, but yes, I suppose I will if I have to. If she agrees."

"Good." Desiree's eyes gleamed with satisfaction as she reached inside her bag and pulled out a small sack. "But for now, make sure she drinks a cup of this tea at least twice a day." She handed him the sack. "I put in enough for you, too." She winked. "More research."

Remy simply shook his head. The old woman was incorrigible.

"Now…" She backed up. "I have to be going. Flora is waiting for me, but I'll check back with you in the morning to see how your woman is getting along. And I'll bring you a fresh change of clothes."

When Remy nodded, Desiree gave him a serene smile, then turned and made her way slowly down the hallway.

WHEN SHE OPENED HER EYES for the second time since she'd been admitted to the clinic, the first thing she saw was Remy Delacroix. But this time, instead of staring at her, he was sprawled in the lounge chair. His head was tilted to one side at a neck-breaking angle and his eyes were closed. The shirt he had on was wrinkled, his hair was in dire need of combing, and his jaw was shadowy with beard. He appeared to be sound asleep.

*My hero,* she thought, a bit amused at catching him napping. *Or could he be the enemy in disguise?*

Her momentary amusement abruptly fled, and she suddenly felt lost and frightened once again.

Was it in her nature to be suspicious or did she have reason to be? she wondered. So far Remy had been nothing but kind. Thinking back, she vaguely recalled him mentioning that he and Desiree had taken turns watching over her during the night. And here he was, still trying to watch over her.

Feeling guilty for her doubts, she glanced toward the single window in the room. The blinds were closed, but she could see daylight peeping through the cracks. She didn't know the exact time, but she figured it was probably late afternoon. No wonder the poor man was asleep. He was probably exhausted, and the reason for his exhaustion was her.

*Your so-called accident wasn't an accident…they left you there, knowing that you would eventually die from exposure.*

A shiver of fear ran through her once more, and tears burned her eyes. Who wanted her dead and why? She bit back a moan of pure frustration. The whole situation was so confusing.

With a soft sigh, she closed her eyes. If only she could remember who she was and what she'd been doing on that island, maybe everything else would make sense.

But for now, she wanted to get up—needed to get up and pay a visit to the connecting bathroom. She opened her eyes and glanced at Remy. Recalling her last humiliating experience, when he'd carried her to the bathroom on his houseboat, she hesitated, weighing her need against taking a chance that he might wake up. Waking him was the last thing she wanted, since it would be just her luck that he would insist on helping her again.

In the end, need won out.

She eyed the buttons that operated the electric

gizmo that could raise or lower the head of the bed. Using it would make getting up much easier, but she was pretty sure the thing would be noisy. Better to try it on her own, she decided.

It was awkward with the cast on her arm, but she was finally able to ease herself to a sitting position and drag her feet over the side of the bed. So far, so good, she thought as she waited to see if she was going to be overcome with dizziness as before. After a moment she began inching herself to the edge of the bed.

The tile floor was cool under her feet when she stood. Her legs were a bit wobbly at first, reminding her of the incident in the boat earlier, but the longer she stood there, the stronger they began to feel. Even so, she was reluctant to let go of the bed rail just yet.

"Do you need some help?"

Her pulse jumped, and she tensed at the unexpected sound of his voice. Leaning against the bed rail and grabbing the gaping edges of her hospital gown with her good hand, she faced him. "I thought you were asleep," she snapped, unnerved at being startled and too aware of how little the skimpy gown covered.

"Just catching a little catnap," he drawled.

"Could have fooled me," she muttered as her throbbing pulse slowed to normal.

"It's an old trick of the trade." He pushed himself out of the chair and stood. "By the way, do the initials J.K.D. mean anything to you?"

She slowly shook her head as she silently repeated the initials several times. "No. Should they?"

"What about the Louisiana Department of Environmental Standards?"

Again, she shook her head. "Sorry, it means nothing. Is it important?"

"I'm not sure yet, but like I said before, do you need some help?"

She was going to question him further, but when he suddenly raised his arms and stretched, twisting first one way, then the other, she could feel the heat of embarrassment rising from her neck to her cheeks, and all coherent thoughts fled.

The knit shirt he wore tightened over his broad chest, outlining well-defined muscles. He reminded her of a sleek, sinewy tiger, wild and beautiful to watch, and something akin to desire snaked through her veins.

She slowly raised her gaze until she was looking into his eyes. Was he also as dangerous as a tiger could be?

# CHAPTER FIVE

IT WAS AS IF TIME switched into slow motion, then stopped as they stared at each other. A sensual energy seemed to crackle in the air between them, and from the wide-eyed look in his mystery woman's face and her flushed cheeks, Remy knew she felt it, too. When he'd stretched, he'd felt her eyes on him like caressing, invisible fingers. Such beautiful eyes, he thought. Warm and inviting, yet mysterious, like the woman herself.

As if his legs had a mind of their own, Remy found himself moving toward her. Then he was facing her, just inches away.

"Why didn't you ask for help?"

"I didn't…" Her flushed cheeks turned a darker pink. "I mean, I thought you were asleep and I didn't want to disturb you."

Her soft voice was husky, a sure sign that he hadn't simply imagined the past few unsettling moments, and *disturb* was far too tame a word to describe what she did to him.

"I need to…" Her cheeks turned a darker pink as she cleared her throat and lifted her chin a notch. "Nature calls," she said bluntly. "And I want to brush my teeth and take a shower."

He hadn't imagined the last few minutes—he was

sure of it. But her words brought him back to reality with a jolt.

Plain and simple, she had been too embarrassed to ask for his help. And why wouldn't she be? He was a man, and almost a perfect stranger. Then out of nowhere, something deep inside of him stirred, feelings he recognized as sympathy and tenderness—emotions he hadn't experienced for a very long time.

"Would you feel more comfortable if I called for a nurse to help you?" he asked softly.

The look of relief in her eyes was all the answer he needed.

Minutes later, Remy watched as Janet Brousard, one of the nurse's aides, placed her arm around his mystery lady's waist and escorted her to the bathroom. His lady was still self-consciously clutching the back of her hospital gown when the aide shut the door.

Independent and modest, he thought. Her identity might be a mystery, but he was beginning to get a handle on her personality. Evidently her memory loss didn't include loss of certain innate character traits.

Remy sighed and walked over to the food tray that Janet had brought with her. He absently lifted the cover. There was a bowl of steaming chicken noodle soup, crackers, a container of applesauce and milk.

He personally didn't think any of it looked very appetizing, but the aroma of the soup reminded him that it had been a long time since his last meal, and it also reminded him of the tea that Desiree had given him.

He glanced at his watch. If memory served him, the small cafeteria shut down around seven. If he left now, he should have time to call Claudia, then grab something to eat before it closed.

Remy walked over to the bathroom door and rapped lightly. He could hear water running, and it was a minute before the door opened just enough for Janet to stick her head out. "Yes?"

"Is she okay?"

The aide nodded. "She's fine."

"Will you please tell her that I'm leaving for a few minutes, but I'll be back?"

Again the older woman nodded, then smiled knowingly and shut the door.

WHEN CLAUDIA ANSWERED the phone, Remy could tell she was just as edgy as she'd been when he'd talked to her earlier. "What's wrong, Claudia? Has your brother been around again?"

"Nope, I ain't seen him today, thank the Lord. It's just been one heck of a crazy day."

Remy wasn't sure he believed her entirely. Claudia could have some harebrained idea that if she admitted that Joey had shown up again and caused another scene, Remy might fire her, as her last two bosses had done. So for the moment, he decided to drop the subject. Nevertheless, he figured it was past time to have a little heart-to-heart with Claudia's brother. Like most bullies, the man just needed someone to stand up to him, Remy figured, and though normally he made it a rule not to interfere in his employees' lives, Claudia was the exception. He had a vested interest in her well-being. Not only was she one of the most dependable and valued employees he had, but with his encouragement, she was trying to further

her education, something her ignorant family would never understand. All they saw in her was free maid service—someone to cook and clean up after them.

"Did Ray bring in the rental boat?" Remy asked, pulling his thoughts back to the problems of the moment.

"Yeah. He got back a few minutes after we talked this morning."

"That's good," he replied. "Now, how about that license plate number I asked you to get?"

"Remy, what the heck's going on? First the rental boat and the woman, then that DES stuff, and now this license business. You gonna level with me or what?"

"Look, I promise I'll fill you in later, but for now, I need to know if there was a car left sitting in that parking lot, and if there was, I need the license number."

He could hear Claudia's sigh across the phone line. "Okay, Remy. I reckon you're the boss. There's a car still parked out there," she said. "You got a pen and paper this time?"

Remy chuckled. "Touché! Yes, I do, so shoot."

He jotted down the number and make of the automobile that Claudia read to him. "Thanks," he said when he'd finished, "and I promise I'll fill you in soon. But for now, keep the place running for me for a few days, will you? I'll be busy, but I'll check in with you from time to time in case there are any problems. And by the way, I almost forgot that Thursday is Thanksgiving. You haven't booked any tours that day, have you?"

"No. I remembered not to."

"Great! And thanks again." His nerves humming with anticipation, Remy hung up.

Hoping to catch his niece before she left for the day so she could run a make on the license, he immediately placed a call to the police academy, only to be told that Charly had already left. With a sigh of frustration, he called her apartment.

"Make it fast, oh, ancient uncle of mine," his niece quipped. "My hair is dripping wet, and I've got a hot date with a blow drier before I go to work."

Remy grinned. Charly was the youngest of his nieces, as well as his favorite, and he could always count on her to make him smile. "Far be it from me to keep you from a hot date, but I need another favor. When you get to work, can you run a license plate for me?"

"Tonight?"

"No," he drawled. "Yesterday."

"That's what I was afraid you were going to say. Want to clue me in first?"

"Nope, not yet."

"Hmm, it's a good thing you're my favorite uncle. Give me the numbers and give me about an hour."

REMY'S NEXT STOP was the cafeteria, where he wolfed down a hamburger that tasted like it had been swimming in grease all day, then washed it down with a glass of milk.

By the time he'd persuaded one of the cafeteria workers to brew him a cup of Desiree's tea and he'd returned to his mystery lady's room, his nerves were stretched tighter than the strings on a Cajun fiddle.

Remy hesitated at the door of the hospital room.

Up until now, he had just barged in without knocking, but that was before she was fully conscious and getting around on her own. He should probably knock, but what if she was asleep? With a shrug, he eased the door open, taking care to be as quiet as possible.

The second he spotted her standing by the window, he froze in his tracks.

Her back was to him, and she was so self-absorbed as she stared out the window into the darkness that she was totally unaware that he had opened the door. But it was the thin, skimpy hospital gown she wore that drew his attention. It was held together loosely by a tie and did nothing to hide her bare back or shapely behind.

Recalling her earlier show of modesty, Remy stepped backward and eased the door shut. But not even the solid wooden door could block out the image of her standing there—an image that was burned into his mind, playing havoc with his libido.

Pajamas, he thought. Or a gown. One of those thick cotton kinds that cover everything. First thing the following morning, he'd have to see about getting her one. For her sake as well as his.

Swallowing hard and straightening his shoulders, he rapped lightly on the door, then waited until he heard her muted voice call out, "Come in."

When he opened the door this time, she was sitting in the bed, a sheet pulled up and tucked beneath her arms.

Remy cleared his throat. "I brought you something, compliments of Desiree." He walked to the bed and held out the foam cup.

"What's in it?" she asked as she took it and gingerly peeled off the lid.

"Tea. Probably something she blended just for you, I imagine."

She sniffed the steam rising out of the cup. "Umm, it smells wonderful, but when did you see Desiree?" She took a tentative sip.

"She dropped by earlier to check on you, but you were still sleeping."

"This tastes as good as it smells, but..." the woman raised her gaze and looked him straight in the eyes. "Why?" she asked bluntly. "I don't mean to sound ungrateful, but why is she being so nice to me and why are you still here?"

Her questions were reasonable. Even so, he was at a loss for an answer. Explaining Desiree's interest was easy enough, but how could he explain his own? How could he explain something he didn't really understand himself?

"Desiree considers you one of her patients," he finally answered. "As I've said before, some believe she's a white witch, and she's highly respected for her healing powers throughout the bayou, I might add. She even saved my father and my uncle once, when they were sick with a fever as children."

He was babbling, talking on and on in order to avoid her question. Time to exit, he thought.

Remy made a show of glancing at his watch and began backing toward the door. "Right now, I have to make another phone call, but when I come back, we'll talk some more."

She didn't say anything, but she didn't have to. The knowing look in her eyes told him that he wasn't fooling her for one second. They both knew that he had answered only part of her question.

Remy turned and hurried out of the room. All he could do now was hope that Charly had been able to trace the license plate and that he'd have some real answers for his mystery lady when he returned.

IN THE HALL where the pay phone was located, Remy paced back and forth. It hadn't been quite an hour since he'd talked with Charly, and he wanted to give her plenty of time, but...

"To hell with it," he muttered, digging in his pocket for a quarter. Seconds later, he had his niece on the line. "What did you find out?"

"Uncle Remy, just what are you up to?"

"Charly?"

"Okay, okay. It's a company car, but not just any company. It belongs to the State of Louisiana and is registered to the DES—that's the Department—"

"I know what it stands for!" Remy snapped. "Are you absolutely sure that there's no name, just the agency?"

The silence on the other end of the line was deafening, and calling himself names that wouldn't bear repeating out loud, Remy closed his eyes. Back to square one, he thought, suddenly more tired than he'd felt in a long time. But venting his disappointment on his niece was inexcusable. "Look, Charly, I'm sorry. I didn't mean to take your head off."

When several seconds ticked by and Charly still hadn't spoken, Remy tried again. "I said I'm sorry. What more do you want?"

"Ah-ha, I thought you'd never ask. You see, after

tonight, I have a few days off, and there's this really cool pair of leather boots at the Bayou Boutique that I've had my eye on for several days now.''

Remy knew instantly he'd been had, and some of his anger melted. Even as a child, Charly had been able to wrap him around her little finger. ''Sounds like a bribe to me.''

''You bet your sweet a—''

''Watch it, little girl.''

''Oops! Sorry. But really, Uncle Remy, in case you haven't noticed, I haven't been a little girl for a long time now.''

Remy leaned against the wall and stared up at the ceiling. He'd noticed, all right, but all noticing did was make him feel old. ''Tell you what. Go pick up your boots, and while you're at it, pick out a nice conservative nightgown for me—the kind that leaves everything to the imagination. I need a size small and it's got to have loose sleeves. Have them send the bill to the gift shop and deliver the nightgown to the medical clinic, room 101.''

''Since when did you get into cross-dressing? And what are you doing at the clinic?''

''Behave yourself, Charly. It's for a friend of mine who happens to be a patient. Now, do you want your boots or not?''

''Guess that means I should stop asking questions, huh?''

''Tomorrow,'' he answered. ''Have them deliver the gown first thing tomorrow morning. And by the way, thanks for your help.''

''Sure, anytime. But aren't you going to tell me what this is all about?''

"Goodbye, Charly."

Remy hung up the receiver and rolled his eyes. Now what? he wondered. Though it was a long shot, there was still the possibility that a fingerprint check might turn up the identity of his mystery lady, but that could take up to two weeks.

He scowled. Just what in blazes was he going to do with her until then?

Remy cursed. He knew exactly what he had to do; he'd just been hoping it wouldn't be necessary. He'd have to take her home with him.

*And what if she refuses to go with you?* his cynical inner voice taunted.

*She won't,* he silently argued. But he'd cross that bridge when he got there. Somehow he'd find a way to persuade her.

Dragging his feet, he headed back down the hallway. With any luck, she would be asleep by now and he could wait until morning to broach the subject.

Remy hesitated at the door and began to mentally rehearse what to say to her. The way his luck was running, he figured he'd best be prepared to make his pitch even if he did feel like death warmed over.

But when he finally entered, the room was dark, lit only by an outside streetlight shining through the open blinds. Remy stepped closer to the bed. Her breathing was soft and even, and once again she had curled up on her side. As best he could tell, she was asleep.

He walked around the foot of the bed and eyed the lounge chair. It wouldn't be the most comfortable night he'd ever spent, but it wouldn't be the worst, either.

*SHE WAS LYING in a pool of blood, staring up at him, her eyes wild with pain and confusion. "Help me, Remy! Please don't let me die. Oh, God! Remy... please..."*

Remy awoke with a start, his body bathed in cold sweat. Pushing himself up in the chair, he twisted his head to relieve his cramped neck and tried to clear his head enough to think.

No matter how real it had seemed, it was just a dream, he kept telling himself, another of the many nightmares he'd had for months after Julie's death.

So what had triggered the recurring dream this time?

He cut his eyes toward the hospital bed, but the room was so dark he could barely make out the small mound of his mystery woman's sheet-draped body.

"No...! Please..."

The sudden sound of her voice brought him instantly alert and he jumped to his feet. In two strides, he ate up the distance between the chair and her bed.

"Help me!" Her voice was a shrill cry of terror as she tried to get up, the same cry of help he'd heard in his disturbing dream.

"Hey, it's okay," he said soothingly, grasping her shoulder with one hand in an attempt to restrain her. With his other hand, he fumbled above the bed for the cord connected to the light switch.

"No...don't!" she cried, striking out blindly with her good arm and catching his chin with a glancing blow.

*Stay calm,* he told himself, still grappling for the light-switch cord. "Come on, sweetheart, stop fighting me!" When his fingers finally connected with the cord, he gave a quick yank and light flooded the room.

But not even the light seemed to penetrate the nightmarish struggle she was caught in, for she continued to thrash around. Afraid she was going to hurt herself, Remy took hold of her wrist and, careful of her broken arm, pinned her against the mattress, using his body as a restraint. "Come on, honey, wake up. It's only a dream."

For a moment more she fought him, then she suddenly went still.

For seconds, neither of them moved and the only sound in the room was her harsh breathing. With his upper body pressed intimately against hers, he could feel each beat of her pounding heart.

"You—you can get off me now. I—I'm awake."

Remy heard her, but his body seemed to have a mind of its own. It was when he began to realize that the lower part of his body also seemed to have a mind of its own that he came to his senses.

He eased up off of her, but when he'd pulled away enough to see her face, what he'd planned to say died in his throat. Her eyes were squeezed tightly shut, but not tightly enough to keep tears from streaming down her cheeks.

"Hey, it's okay." He cupped her cheek, his thumb gently brushing at the tears.

"S-sorry," she whispered. "I—I..." Suddenly she cried out. It was a heart-wrenching sound that shook Remy clear to his soul.

In one swift motion, he nudged her hips over so that he could sit on the edge of the bed, then hauled her up against him. Wrapping his arms tightly around her waist, he held her, gently rocking back and forth as deep sobs racked her body.

"I—I'm sorry," she cried over and over, clinging to him with her uninjured arm, so fiercely that he could feel her fingernails digging into his back. "If—if only I could remember my name or where I came from, I—I'm sure I could remember the rest."

Each word was like a hammer blow, chipping away at the armor he'd carefully built around his emotions, and he ached for her in a way that he hadn't felt in a long, long time.

"Maybe you're trying too hard," he offered lamely, at a loss as to exactly what he should or could say to comfort her. "Maybe if you'd just try to relax…"

She pulled away from him. "How can I? I have no memory, no money, no clothes—nothing! And even worse, someone tried to murder me. Why, I could be someone horrible!" She lowered her gaze. "Even a criminal," she said hesitantly.

Remy shook his head, but before he could voice a protest, she continued. "Or what if I have a family—a husband or children somewhere who are worried sick about me? You can't imagine how it feels to be a—a…to be a nobody," she whispered. "A nonperson…" Her voice trailed away.

"No, I can't," he honestly admitted, his voice soft and sympathetic. "But I don't believe you're some kind of criminal or mixed up in any criminal activity. You could have simply been in the wrong place at the wrong time. Hell, who knows, maybe you were even kidnapped." He took her by the shoulders and forced her to look at him. "I've been checking up on some things, and we'll get to the bottom of this sooner or later—I promise. But meantime, you're going to have to be patient and concentrate on getting well."

"You're right...I guess." She sniffed and pulled away. "But shouldn't we notify the authorities, the police?"

Remy hesitated only a moment. "No!" He shook his head vehemently. "No law."

Her eyes widened, and the look in them turned wary, almost distrustful. "But why not?" she demanded. "Surely the police have the means to find out my identity, and if someone tried to kill me once, he might try again. I want to know who did this to me and why. And I want protection."

Remy glared at her. "The police can't do anything I haven't already done," he said, his tone a bit sharper than he'd intended. "If I were you, I wouldn't trust anyone at this point, including the law. And I should know. Before I was a swamp-tour guide, I was on the New Orleans police force for almost twenty years. Ten of those twenty years, I was a police detective, so I'm more than capable of watching over you. What's more, the fewer people who know about you, the better chance you have of staying alive."

# CHAPTER SIX

IF I WERE YOU, I *wouldn't trust anyone....* Remy's harsh words echoed in her head. Chills of terror chased along her spine, and she began to feel queasy.

Should she believe what he was telling her? Or should she insist on calling the police? As for not trusting anyone, did that include him?

For the hundredth time, she wondered why he had appointed himself as her protector. When she'd asked him previously, he'd avoided answering. Avoided answering on purpose, she suspected, by the way he'd acted. But what reason would he have to evade answering her? She could ask him again, but she figured he'd just dance around the subject like he'd done before.

Then she suddenly remembered something he had mentioned earlier. "You said you had been checking on some things."

"I followed up on a couple of leads, but they didn't pan out."

She gritted her teeth in frustration. The man could be so tight-lipped at times that it was like pulling teeth to get information out of him. "What kind of leads?" she pressed insistently.

"The reason I found you in the first place was because I spotted one of my rental boats floating around Willow Island." Remy went on to explain about the logbook and the car left in the parking lot. "Both facts indicate there's a good possibility you work for the DES—the Louisiana Department of Environmental Standards."

For seconds she simply stared at him, and as before, she turned the name over in her mind several times, hoping it would spark some kind of memory.

Still nothing, she realized. The past was a blank. "What makes you think that I work for the government?" she finally asked.

"I'm not positive that you do, but all the evidence points in that direction."

Suddenly, excitement hummed in her veins. "Then all we have to do is call them and give them a description of me. Surely they would recognize one of their employees."

Remy shook his head. "Been there, tried that. No sale. The man in charge is out with the flu and won't be back until after the holidays."

"How convenient," she muttered sarcastically. Disappointment was swift and painful. "Which holiday and when?"

"Day after tomorrow—Thursday—is Thanksgiving."

"Thanksgiving," she repeated absently.

"Yeah, you know, turkey and all the trimmings?"

He wasn't being sarcastic. He'd spoken in earnest, but it was as if he'd touched a raw nerve and she glared at him. "I know what Thanksgiving is," she retorted sharply. "I just don't know who I am or what the devil I was doing on some godforsaken swamp island."

Remy threw up his hands. "Okay, okay! Sorry. Let's just stay calm here."

Instant remorse washed through her for being so testy. She might be suspicious of his motives for helping her, but the fact remained that he was trying, and he had, in fact, probably saved her life. "No," she said evenly. "I'm the one who should apologize." She paused, and for a second considered suggesting again that they call the police. But after the way he'd overreacted before, she decided against doing so. "Is there anything else that can be done?"

"There is, but it's a long shot, and by the time we could get an answer, I should be able to contact the head of the DES."

A grim smile pulled at her lips. "Hey, time seems to be the only thing I have plenty of. I suggest we cover all the bases. So what exactly is the other option?"

"Fingerprints. But running a fingerprint check could take a while, and even then there are no guarantees."

"Guarantees or not, at this point I'm willing to try anything."

He nodded. "Okay, first thing in the morning we'll take your prints. But there's something else I need to discuss with you."

What now? she wondered, not liking the grim look on his face.

"When Sam releases you, I..." He glanced up at the ceiling and sighed heavily. Then he met her gaze again. "I want you to come home with me, back to the houseboat."

Suddenly she found it hard to breathe. It wasn't

so much the reluctance she detected in his tone and attitude, but it was what he'd asked that had her nerves instantly jumping.

During all the time she'd worried and fretted about her dilemma, she'd been so caught up in trying to figure out who she was that she truly hadn't considered what would happen to her if she didn't regain her memory by the time she left the clinic—where she would go or how she would survive.

"What normally happens to people like me?" she asked. Surely there was some kind of provision made.

"Since we aren't reporting the incident to the police, what normally happens is irrelevant in your case. The—"

"Please, just answer the question," she insisted, feeling her patience slip.

"One of two things: they're either shipped off to a shelter," he said evenly, "or put up in a motel until their identity can be determined."

A shudder rippled through her. More strangers. Yet another unfamiliar place.

"Look," he continued stubbornly, "the houseboat is isolated. No one will bother you there. Even if the person who assaulted you finds out you're still alive and decides to do something about it, there's no way anyone can get near my houseboat without me knowing it. You'll be safe there."

*Safe?* She squirmed uncomfortably. But safe from whom? She didn't know much about Remy Delacroix other than what he'd told her, but there were some things a person sensed. From the beginning she'd sensed that he could be a dangerous man to have for an enemy, the kind who could handle himself under any circumstances. There was a streetsmart toughness about him. On one level, he disturbed her greatly, but on an entirely different level, she felt safe and protected when he was near.

She freely admitted that something about him frightened her. But she was more frightened of the crazy person who had tried to kill her than of Remy. And going with him held a lot more appeal than being thrust in the midst of strangers.

*Better the devil you know.* The cliché popped into her head from out of nowhere, and she wondered if her subconscious was trying to tell her something.

"Okay, I'll go with you," she finally decided.

He said nothing, but simply nodded, and there was nothing in his expression to give her a clue as to whether he was glad she'd agreed or whether he was disappointed. Even though he'd asked her to go home with him, almost insisted, she sensed that he'd only done so because there was no other choice. He wasn't comfortable with the idea. The man was an enigma, she finally decided, and an expert at hiding his emotions.

He eased off the bed. "Why don't you try and get some sleep now?" Without waiting for an answer, he reached behind her and jerked the light cord.

The room was instantly plunged into darkness and she blinked several times. She sensed more than heard him move away, and for a moment she panicked, wondering if he was going to leave her alone in the room. But before her eyes could adjust to the dark, the crackle of the vinyl lounge chair confirmed that he had once again taken up his post of watching over her.

With a soft sigh of relief, she scooted down in the bed. Given her heavy cast and the throbbing in her head, finding a comfortable position was almost impossible, but she finally settled on her back.

As she stared up at the dark ceiling, she tried to clear her mind by concentrating on breathing in and out evenly. She kept hoping that if she could relax enough, her memory might return. But no matter how many deep breaths she took, clearing her mind proved to be impossible and certain stubborn thoughts persisted.

*Your so-called accident wasn't an accident. They left you there to die....*

A shudder rippled through her. Concentrate on something else, she ordered.

As if conjured up by an invisible entity, a larger-than-life image of Remy began to fill her mind—his face rawboned and rugged, his voice deep and raspy.... She recalled the way his body, so hard and fit, had felt pressed against her own when he'd held her close and tried to comfort her, and as she finally drifted off to sleep, the scent of him—a mixture of musk and male—seemed to fill her dreams.

WHEN SHE AWOKE, sunlight streamed into the room and noises filtered through the closed door.

Even before she turned her head, she somehow already knew she would find the lounge chair empty. So where was he? she wondered.

An hour later, as she picked at the food on a breakfast tray that had been brought to her, she was still wondering. Like the evening before, she found eating to be a chore. She was attempting to scoop up a forkful of scrambled eggs when the reason for her awkwardness suddenly dawned on her. She was right-handed, and eating was difficult because she was having to use her left hand.

She dropped the fork and shoved the table holding the tray away. Just one more thing to contend with, she thought, eyeing the cast on her right arm.

A squawking outside the window caught her attention. Two blue jays were chasing each other. Welcoming the diversion, she watched and was soon so enthralled with their antics that when the door suddenly swung open, she let out a yelp of surprise.

"Didn't mean to startle you." With a wide, toothy smile, the aide named Janet bustled into the room. Tucked under one arm was a paper sack and under her other one, a large rectangular box. She placed the box at the foot of the bed. "This was left at the nurse's station for you, and since I need to take your temp and BP, anyway, I volunteered to deliver it." She held out the sack. "And here are your clothes. I hope you don't mind, but as a favor to Remy, I took them home with me last night and washed them." She set the sack on a nearby table.

"Oh, Janet, I—I don't know what to say except thanks."

The aide smiled. "No problem. Remy is an old friend, and I was glad to do it." She motioned to the box. "As for that..." Her eyes danced with mischief. "I'm dying to know what's inside, since it came from the Bayou Boutique. But first things first." She pressed a button to adjust the head of the bed, then produced a thermometer.

Obediently opening her mouth, then holding the thermometer under her tongue, she eyed the box with curiosity while the aide took her blood pressure. Since no one but the clinic staff knew about her or her situation, the gift had to have come from either Remy, the doctor or Desiree. So which one had sent it? she wondered, her curiosity growing with each passing minute. And what was in it?

The thermometer began beeping, and Janet removed it. "Okay, my dear," she said as she jotted down the results on a chart. "Let's see what's in that box." She placed it in her patient's lap.

Sitting straight up in the bed, she lifted the lid, pulled away the tissue paper and saw what she'd uncovered, her breath caught in her throat. "Oh, my!" With eager fingers she pulled it out, and the aide whisked the box away.

The gown was made from yards and yards of flowing, gauzy cotton. It had loose sleeves, a scalloped, lace-trimmed neckline, tiny pearl buttons down the bodice and an ankle-length flounced hem. Best of all, it was roomy enough to slip over her head without having to worry about the buttons.

"Is there a card?" she asked, still unable to take her eyes off the gown.

Janet rummaged through the box, then shook her head. "No card."

A sigh escaped her lips as she fingered the soft material. The gown was certainly beautiful in a feminine, romantic way, and just the thought of having something—anything—besides the hospital gown to wear was heaven. So why was she suddenly wishing for an oversize T-shirt?

Gathering up the gown, she swung her legs over the side of the bed. "I want a shower."

WHEN REMY KNOCKED on the door a few minutes later, there was no response. A myriad of thoughts suddenly rushed through his head. What if she'd fainted or slipped and hit her head? After a moment's hesitation, he pushed open the door and entered the hospital room. At the sight of the empty bed, he immediately tensed. His hand tightened around the rolled-up wildlife magazine he'd picked up in the waiting room.

Then the sound of running water penetrated his awareness, and he swung around to stare at the closed bathroom door.

With a sigh of relief, he shoved his fingers through his hair and walked to the lounge chair. Where his mystery lady was concerned, he was entirely too jumpy, he decided, too ready to overreact. But what concerned him even more was that he could feel himself losing the steel control over his emotions that he'd so carefully nurtured since he'd left his police career behind...since Julie's death.

*No,* he silently corrected himself. *Julie didn't simply die. She was murdered.*

*And what if it happens again? What if you can't prevent the murder of this woman, just like you couldn't prevent Julie's?*

Remy felt his gut tighten at the unsettling thought. Was that the reason he'd felt so drawn to his mystery lady in the first place? Was that what had brought about all of these unfamiliar, protective feelings? Did he somehow see this as his opportunity to redeem himself…redeem his soul?

Maybe that was part of it, he finally admitted, but only a small part. He couldn't explain it and hadn't wanted to admit it up until now, but he knew deep down that his feelings for his mystery lady ran deeper than that.

Since Remy didn't like to dwell on things he couldn't explain or didn't understand, it was almost a relief when he heard the shower being shut off. When the door to the bathroom finally opened and she walked out, he was mindlessly thumbing through the magazine.

He glanced up, and the magazine slipped from his nerveless fingers and fell to the floor.

On anyone else, the gown would have been modest, even a bit prudish, but on her, it was by far one of the sexiest-looking ones he'd ever seen, and a hell of a lot worse on his libido than the skimpy hospital gown she'd been wearing. He could feel himself growing harder with each passing second.

Remy shifted in the chair, snatched up the magazine and placed it carefully in his lap. "I see that the boutique delivered the gown," he said in a voice that sounded strained even to his own ears.

A pink blush colored her cheeks, and when she offered a soft "Thank you," her voice sounded even more strained than his own. "I—I wondered who had sent it."

Remy felt her embarrassment acutely, and he was seized with a sudden need to explain, to put her at ease. But at that moment, Janet emerged from the bathroom.

"Dr. Sam should be by any minute now," the aide offered brightly, completely oblivious to the sizzling tension between the two other occupants of the room.

As if the mere mention of the doctor's name had conjured him up, there was a short knock at the door, then Sam strolled in, followed closely by the new nurse he had introduced as Nora.

The doctor nodded a brief greeting at Remy before turning his attention to his patient. "Since you're up and about, you must be feeling better," he said with a smile. Not waiting for an answer, he consulted his chart while Janet helped her back into bed.

"I'll be back after a while to check on you," the aide said, before turning and leaving the room.

"Remy, why don't you step outside for a few minutes while I examine our patient?" Sam instructed absently as he made a notation on the chart.

Out in the hallway, Remy slouched against the wall, crossed his arms over his chest and stared up at the ceiling. The minutes seemed to drag by while he waited. He finally shoved away from the wall and began pacing, but stopped abruptly when the door opened.

Sam stuck his head out. "You can come back in now."

Back inside, Sam once again faced his patient, his expression thoughtful. "I know I said I'd keep you in here for a couple of days, but you're doing excellent, and there's been an outbreak of a nasty flu virus in the community. The clinic is filling up fast, and frankly, I need the bed. So…I'm going to release you today, instead.'' He paused to cast Remy a meaningful glance, then shifted his gaze back to his patient. "Do you have somewhere to go?"

After a brief hesitation, she nodded. "Yes, I do."

When a soft knock sounded at the door, all heads turned in that direction.

"Who is it?" Sam snapped, obviously irritated at being interrupted.

The door opened and Desiree entered the room. "It's only me, you young rooster, so watch your tone of voice."

A grim smile pulled at Sam's lips. "My apologies, Ms. Desiree, but we're in the middle of a discussion here, so if you could just wait out—"

"No, I won't wait outside. I'm here to check on my patient." Ignoring Sam's sigh of frustration, she stepped over to Remy and handed him a brown grocery sack. "Clean clothes for you, mon ami," she said, before turning back to Sam. "She was mine first, Samuel. You only got her because I referred her to you."

Remy could tell that Sam was having as much trouble keeping a straight face as he was.

"Now, if you all don't mind," Desiree said imperiously, "I would like to have a few moments alone with my patient."

"Only if I get a hug, you old con artist."

Desiree made a clucking sound, but then a self-satisfied grin spread over her face. "Sticks and stones, Samuel. Sticks and stones." She held out her arms and Sam gently embraced her.

Out in the hallway, Sam sent Nora on her way to check on their next patient. When she was well out of earshot, he turned to Remy. "I gather she's going home with you."

Remy nodded.

"Are you sure that's wise? Hell, man, she could be anybody. And anyone could be after her—from the Mafia to drug dealers. You're leaving yourself wide open and taking a big chance. If something should happen to her—"

"It won't," Remy retorted.

"Why are you being so pigheaded and arrogant about this? Turn her over to Jake and let him handle things!"

Remy shook his head stubbornly. "I'll take care of it."

"Dammit, man, what's with you and this woman?"

Remy didn't respond because he didn't have an answer.

Sam swore. "Well, I don't like it. Not one bit."

"No one says you have to," Remy drawled.

"Look, I know what went down four years ago. I was the one who patched you up, if you remember. And yes, you got a bad deal all the way around, but that was in the city. Dammit, man, this is your home, and the law here is different. Jake isn't like those others."

"So I've heard," Remy answered sarcastically. "If it will make you feel any better, Desiree agrees with you."

"So?"

He simply shrugged. "So nothing. As I said before, I'll take care of it. My turf. My problem."

## CHAPTER SEVEN

BY MIDAFTERNOON Remy's mystery lady found herself seated in the bottom of his boat and wishing she was back in bed.

At the clinic, she'd submitted to Desiree's brief examination more or less to humor the old woman. Afterward, Desiree had taken up residence in the lounge chair and kept her company while Remy ran errands, one of which included obtaining a fingerprint kit.

Once he had taken her fingerprints and Sam had officially released her, she and Remy had made four stops before arriving at the dock where he kept his boat: one to get a pain prescription filled; one at a grocery store; and another at the Bayou Boutique, where he'd insisted she pick out enough clothes to last for several days. She'd made a stab at protesting, but Remy had been adamant.

Having to accept his charity was humiliating, and as she'd tried on the expensive items, she'd vowed that somehow, someday, she would pay back every cent he had spent on her, including her bill at the clinic.

The fourth stop had been the Willow Island Swamp Tours visitors' parking lot, where she'd found herself staring at a late-model Chevrolet. The automobile was dull gray, and nothing about it had struck a familiar chord. Standard government issue, Remy had told her once he'd opened the door with something he called a Slim Jim and given the inside a thorough going-over. She wondered which of them had been more disappointed when his search turned up nothing personal.

Bowing her head now, she closed her eyes against the bright glare of the sun reflecting off the brackish bayou water and covered them with her good hand while Remy loaded the boat with their purchases.

The constant headache she'd been plagued with had lessened to a manageable level at the clinic. But between the bright sunlight and exhaustion, not to mention a case of nerves stretched to the breaking point, the pain had escalated again, and the lunch she'd eaten felt as if it were stuck in the back of her throat.

"Here, take one of these."

She peeked up at Remy through her fingers. In one hand he was holding a pill she recognized as her pain medication, and in his other, a container of bottled water. She took both and eagerly swallowed the pill, washing it down with the water. Now, if only she could keep it down, she thought as a bitter acid taste kept rising in her throat.

"This might help, too." He handed her a white baseball hat emblazoned with Willow Island Swamp Tours in dark green letters, then a pair of sunglasses.

"Thanks," she said, touched by his chivalrous gesture. The hat and sunglasses were both too big, which made her suspect they belonged to Remy. She was able to adjust the hat so it wouldn't put pressure on her injured head, and although there wasn't much she could do about the glasses, she shoved them on, anyway.

A high-pitched shout shattered the muggy air. "Hey, Remy, wait up!"

Remy muttered something she couldn't quite understand, since it sounded almost like a growl, and she glanced up at him. He was standing on the dock, feet spread apart, hands on his narrow hips, and he was glaring toward the small, quaint shack that housed the gift shop.

"What's wrong?" she asked, turning to see who or what had annoyed him.

At first she wasn't sure if the person jogging toward them was male or female, child or adult. Cutoffs and a baggy T-shirt didn't offer any clues.

"It's Claudia," he answered with an impatient sigh. "She's one of my employees. I had hoped to be gone before anyone saw us. Should have known better," he muttered.

Claudia turned out to be a young sprite of a woman with unruly dark hair and an elfin face sprinkled generously with freckles.

"Hey, Remy, what's going on? Why didn't you come inside?"

"Because I'm in a hurry."

Claudia glanced sideways, curiosity written all over her face. Then she did a double-take. "Oh, it's you—the lady Remy was asking about. Hello again."

Having someone actually recognize her was an unnerving experience. It was a stark reminder that just two short days ago, she'd had a name, an identity, a life, and now…now she had nothing but some maniac who was bent on murdering her.

She shivered. Why oh why hadn't she told the young woman her name? she wondered. If she'd only done so, instead of leaving initials, as Remy had explained, she might not be in the predicament she found herself in now.

Unsure of what to say or even if she should say anything, she summoned what she hoped looked like a polite smile, then peered up at Remy for guidance.

He was watching her, watching her reaction to the young woman. Though the expression on his face was guarded, she thought she detected a spark of sympathy in his eyes before he cleared he throat and turned.

"Claudia, I'm kinda in a hurry." His tone was brisk and didn't invite conversation. "We need to be on our way. Was there anything specific you needed to talk to me about?"

Like a Ping-Pong ball, Claudia's gaze bounced between them, finally resting on Remy. A deep flush darkened her freckled cheeks. "Well—er, no," she stammered, stepping backward. "Nothing that can't wait."

"Great, hon," he said, his tone softening somewhat. "We'll talk Friday, then."

"Yeah…sure, Friday." With one more glance at the boat, Claudia shrugged, her eyes wide with questions. "N-nice to see you again." She lifted her hand and gave a funny little wave, then did an about-face. By the time she reached the gift shop, Remy had already cast off, cranked the motor and headed the boat up the bayou.

The first few minutes of the ride were miserable. With her eyes tightly shut, she concentrated on taking deep breaths and prayed that she could hold on to the contents of her stomach so the pain pill could begin working.

It was only when the nausea finally began to subside that she began noticing other things: the rattling call of a kingfisher over the low-pitched drone of the motor; the stiff, hot breeze against her face; the unmistakable scent of lakewater and clean air, heady and definitely familiar.

She breathed deeply and a strange feeling suddenly assailed her. It was a sensation so familiar that she was sure she was on the verge of recalling something, something that might prove to be the very key that could unlock the floodgate of her dammed-up memories.

Like a runaway train, her heart hammered with anticipation. She slowly opened her eyes. Backed by a bright blue sky, and surrounded by dark, muddy water, the towering swamp cypress and black gums flashed by. As the wake from Remy's motor reached them, the trees appeared to be dancing in and out of the shadowy water. But the fleeting memory that had seemed so close faded almost as quickly as it had come, so quickly that she felt like screaming with frustration and disappointment.

Instead, she shoved the oversize sunglasses back up onto the bridge of her nose and squeezed her eyes tightly shut again, blocking out the passing scenery and the bright sun.

*So close, but no brass ring.* The phrase sprang to mind, and once again she felt like screaming.

AS IF THEY'D HAD a mutual unspoken agreement, neither attempted conversation during the boat ride. Remy had seemed preoccupied with his own thoughts, and she hadn't felt up to shouting over the drone of the motor even if she'd had anything to talk about.

Suddenly Remy cut the speed of the engine. Curious, she glanced up to see why, praying that they had finally arrived at their destination. Just the thought of a quiet, dark room, a bed and a soft pillow to lay her head on seemed like heaven.

Up ahead was a houseboat—Remy's home and their destination, she presumed. She'd been in so much pain the day he'd taken her to the clinic that she hadn't paid much attention to her surroundings, but now she saw that his home was nothing like she'd imagined.

It was a fascinating piece of architecture and a lot larger than she'd thought it would be. The oblong, floating building, constructed out of wood that she suspected was a combination of cypress and cedar, was stained a gray-brown color to blend in naturally with its surroundings. A covered porch ran all around the house, and on the deck in front were several lawn chairs, a small, round table and what appeared to be a barbecue grill.

Remy cut the motor completely, and they glided up to the pier.

"You look a little pale," he said as he quickly moored the boat. "Better wait and let me help you out."

She was so tired of feeling out of control and helpless that it was on the tip of her tongue to argue with him, but one look at his stubborn expression made her change her mind.

Inside the houseboat, he didn't waste time, but escorted her straight back to a small bedroom. What she was able to take in as he hurried her along was once again nothing like she had expected. The coordinated furnishings were simple but tasteful, and the neatness of the rooms surprised her, giving her yet another insight into the character of the puzzling, complex man who had appointed himself her protector.

"Sam gave strict instructions that you were to have bed rest for at least a couple more days." He motioned toward the neatly made bed. "So why don't you get settled in while I unload the boat? Then I'll see what I can come up with for dinner."

She sighed heavily. "It seems I'm forever thanking you, but once again, thanks."

Accepting gratitude didn't seem to come easily to her host. Looking a bit ill at ease, he a gave a curt nod before he left the room.

The moment he was out of sight, she collapsed on the bed. But as she drifted off, eager for the blessed relief of sleep, for a split second more qualms assailed her.

Here she was, in the middle of nowhere with a stranger. She had no memory and nothing to call her own.

Had she made the right decision? Or should she have insisted on contacting the police?

Right or wrong, it was too late now, she finally concluded. All she could do for the time being was try to be as little trouble as possible and hope and pray that her memory would return soon.

TWO HOURS LATER, Remy stood in the bedroom doorway and stared at the woman in his bed. All the errands and the ride to the houseboat must have exhausted her more than he'd thought.

Had he done the right thing, insisting that she come home with him, or should he have turned her over to Jake Trahan? If it came right down to it, would Remy be able to protect her, keep her from harm?

With a sigh, he quietly moved away from the door and headed back to the kitchen. Only time would tell if he'd made the right decision. But he'd be a fool to deny being scared. Julie's death had almost destroyed him, but if something happened to his mystery lady, he didn't think he'd survive this time.

In the kitchen, he checked the pot of red beans and sausage that was bubbling on the stove.

Thanks to Desiree, they wouldn't go hungry tonight, he thought as he stirred the food, then turned down the heat beneath the pot.

Remy shook his head. Desiree never ceased to amaze him. Not only had she straightened up the houseboat, but she'd left the beans and a container of cooked rice in his refrigerator, along with instructions, scrawled in her chicken-scratch handwriting, on warming everything.

If it had been up to him, they would have made do with sandwiches, since his idea of cooking was heating up prepared frozen dinners out of the grocery store or dropping by the Bayou Inn.

Remy stepped out onto the deck. Gripping the railing, he leaned forward and braced himself as he drew in a deep gulp of the humid air. Should he awaken his mystery lady so that she could eat, or did she need sleep more than food?

Night was creeping across the bayou, and the only sounds were the splash of fish rising to catch insects, the far-off hooting of a barred owl and an occasional bellow from an alligator that had strayed from its winter nest.

Remy wasn't sure how long he'd been standing there when, from out of nowhere, an alien noise echoed across the still waters. He quickly identified the sound as the purr of an outboard motor.

He tensed. For a split second he wondered if it was possible that the perp who had assaulted the woman had somehow found out she was still alive. Even now, he could be on his way to try and finish her off.

Almost as soon as the thought entered his head, Remy dismissed it. Only a handful of people knew about her, so the chances that the boat belonged to the perp were slim to none.

Remy frowned. Most of the locals knew better than to be prowling the swamps at night, so who else was stupid enough to be out there? he wondered.

Suddenly he ground his teeth in frustration. The answer was so obvious that if it had been a snake, it would have bitten him. He'd been so wrapped up in the woman that he'd completely forgotten about the poacher. More than likely the bastard was up to his old tricks again.

Remy cursed. Since sounds traveled a long way

over the water, there was no way of pinpointing an exact location, and there was nothing he could do about it until morning, anyway. By then it would be too late; the poacher would be long gone. With the Fish and Wildlife regulations so tight, Remy still hadn't figured out what the creep was doing with the alligator skins. It was possible that the poacher had found some way to smuggle them out of the country, but until he actually caught him, it was useless to speculate.

Remy pushed away from the railing and returned to the kitchen just in time to hear the beep of the microwave. He removed the cooked rice Desiree had left, checked the beans once again, then switched off the burner.

Suddenly, a prickly feeling danced down his neck and a jolt of awareness swept over him. Sensing that he was no longer alone, he found his breath frozen in his lungs.

"That smells wonderful," she said from the doorway.

At the sound of her voice, Remy sucked in air, and bit by bit, his tense muscles relaxed.

By the time he glanced over his shoulder, his heart had once more slowed to normal. One look at her was all it took for it to speed up again. She was still dressed in the clothes she'd had on when they'd left the clinic, but now she looked rumpled, sleepy and sexy as hell standing there, leaning against the door frame.

Remy abruptly turned his attention back to the beans. "Compliments of Desiree," he said gruffly, hoping that what he'd been thinking hadn't showed on his face or any other part of his anatomy. *Sexy* was most definitely not a word he should be using to describe his guest, especially given their present circumstances. "I was just debating on whether to wake you or let you keep sleeping."

He felt, rather than heard, her step farther into the room. "Actually, I think it was my stomach growling that woke me." She glanced around. "So what can I do to help?"

It was on the tip of his tongue to deny that he needed help and to insist that she climb back into the bed. But one glimpse of the eager expression on her face made him change his mind.

He might not know anything about her or her background, but he recognized the need to maintain a semblance of self-esteem when he saw it. Whoever she was, one thing was obvious—she didn't feel comfortable freeloading. Not back at the boutique when he'd bought her clothes, and not now. She needed to keep busy and feel as if she were contributing in some way.

He tilted his head toward the cabinet to his right. "Plates and glasses are in there, and forks are in the drawer below."

The look of gratitude in her eyes before she turned away told him he'd guessed right. And for the first time since he'd discovered she had amnesia, he really thought about what it meant. What if the situation was reversed? What if he had been the one who had lost his past, his identity? How would he have handled it if he were in her shoes?

The thought was chilling and he decided he wouldn't be able to handle it, not even half as well as she was coping.

Dinner started out as a quiet affair. He'd just taken his first bite of food when he glanced across the table to see her spill a forkful of beans and rice down the front of her shirt—his shirt.

"I give up!" she muttered as she dropped the fork onto the table, then carefully brushed the food from the shirt.

. He raised one eyebrow.

"This miserable cast...!" She pointed at the plaster encasing her right arm. "I've discovered that I'm right-handed, and having to use my left hand to eat, brush my teeth, comb my hair and all the rest of the ordinary things most people take for granted is almost impossible."

It was as if her sudden burst of temper served as a release valve for her frustration. Glaring at the fork, she sighed. Then, stretching her lips into a firm, thin line of determination, she reached out and picked it up again.

Watching her eat was almost a painful experience, but Remy admired her tenacity. She wasn't a quitter. Still, more than once during the meal, he found himself sorely tempted to take the utensil away from her and feed her himself. Since he doubted she would allow such a thing, he thought better of the idea and concentrated on his own meal.

When she had finally scraped up the last bite, then chewed and swallowed, she held out the fork, a gloating look of triumph on her face. "Sir fork, I dub thee conquered, once and for all." Then she broke into a self-conscious giggle.

The giggle was infectious, and Remy found himself laughing along with her. Given her present lighthearted mood, he figured now was as good a time as any to broach something he'd been thinking about since they'd left the clinic.

"By the way," he said, a grin still on his lips, "I think it's high time we gave you a name. I can't keep calling you 'hey you,' so how about it?"

"Hmm…" She glanced up at the ceiling as if giving the notion serious thought, then nodded. "Actually, I think that's a great idea. So…got anything in mind?"

As he stared into her bright, eager eyes, the lyrics and melody of an old song began playing in his head.

*"Beautiful, beautiful brown eyes…"*

From the beginning, each time he'd looked into those eyes, they had reminded him of a startled, frightened doe. Remy swallowed with difficulty, suddenly uncomfortable. *Can't call her Brown Eyes,* he thought. Too personal…she could get the wrong idea.

*And she would be right.*

Remy ignored the intrusive thought. "How about Jane?" he finally said.

"As in Jane Doe?" she squeaked. "But that's for—for…"

Remy nodded gravely. "Under normal circumstances. But you've defied the odds, and—" he wiggled his eyebrows, à la Groucho Marx "—you look pretty alive to me. Besides…" He leaned forward as if confiding a secret. "Personally, between you and me, I think the name gets a bad rap."

She was staring at him, and Remy found himself not only feeling like a fool, but holding his breath while he waited for her response. Then a twinkle of amusement appeared in her eyes, and she tilted her chin upward. "Why, I believe you're absolutely correct," she said in a fake, haughty tone. "Jane Doe does get a bad rap, and it's time to correct it, to rebel against the establishment. I'd be proud to wear the name, sir."

Remy grinned. "Well, Miz Jane," he drawled, playing along and imitating her exaggerated accent, "if you'll kindly crawl back into the bed, this here rebel has drawn KP duty."

With a smile still on her lips, she stood. "I'd protest, but..." She tapped lightly on the cast encasing her broken arm. "I don't think Dr. Sam would approve of me soaking his handiwork in dishwater."

She was almost to the doorway when he remembered the other matter he'd meant to discuss with her.

"Jane?" he called out.

She paused.

"I might be gone in the morning by the time you wake up," he said. "But I won't be long. I want to get those fingerprints to my niece, and I need to see one of my cousins on another matter. Will you be okay here by yourself?"

She faced him. "I'll be fine."

"I can call Desiree to come stay with you if you'd like."

She shook her head. "No, that's not necessary. I'm sure Desiree has better things to do on Thanksgiving Day than to baby-sit me. Besides, I don't want to be any trouble..." A deep flush stole over her cheeks. "No more trouble than I've already been. But thanks, anyway."

Later, in the narrow solitary bed in the cramped

spare room, Remy stared into the darkness and listened to the night. Always before, being surrounded by the swamp had acted as a balm to soothe and relax him. He could lose himself in its raw beauty—the sights and sounds of it—and forget his troubles. But not tonight.

He shifted restlessly, then flipped over onto his stomach. Only one thin wall separated him from Jane, doing nothing to block out thoughts of her. And like a guilty conscience, images of her nagged at him—images of how she'd looked dressed in the gown he'd bought her...of her curled up in his bed, all soft and warm....

REMY AWOKE WITH A START. The room was flooded with daylight. He reached out and snagged his wristwatch off the bedside table. Squinting, he checked the time and cursed. He'd overslept.

He rubbed his eyes, then glared up at the ceiling. Too many nights with too few hours of sleep had finally caught up with him, and last night was no exception, he thought wearily, recalling how he'd tossed and turned.

And now he would have to pay the price. Remy groaned and pinched the bridge of his nose. He'd have to face family members he'd rather not see or deal with...including his father.

As far back as he could remember, his family had always gathered at his aunt Mary's home for holidays and special occasions. Despite his aunt's recent heart attack, today would be no exception. What he'd hoped to do was drop by early before the whole clan arrived.

He'd intended to pay his respects to his aunt, then ask her to give Charly a package containing the fingerprints. And he'd been counting on his cousin Joanna being there early, as usual, helping his aunt. Even though she had been unable to stomach some of her father's practices and had severed professional ties with Philip's law firm to work for his twin brother, Remy's father, Joanna would either know what was behind the survey stakes or could find out.

"Wonderful," he muttered sarcastically. "Just wonderful." It was almost nine now, and by the time he dressed, boated to shore and drove to his aunt's home, a lot of the family would already have arrived.

Suddenly, an earsplitting scream jolted Remy clear to his toes.

"Remy! Help!"

He jackknifed out of bed, yanked on his jeans and tore through the house.

"Remy!"

Jane's second cry helped him pinpoint her location, and by the time he reached the kitchen door leading onto the deck, his heart was pounding like a jackhammer.

Not sure what he might have to face, he crouched, ready to spring into action, as he cautiously eased the door open. The first thing he saw was Jane balanced precariously on top of the patio table at the corner of the porch.

"What the hell," he muttered.

Then he spotted the reason she'd screamed. Blocking her way to safety was an alligator sprawled on the deck.

"It's okay," he called out. "It's only Barney. Just stay where you are and he won't bother you."

"Barney?" she squeaked. "You mean that thing has a name?"

"Just stay there," Remy repeated firmly. Sighing in relief and willing his heart to slow down, he rummaged through the kitchen cabinets. He finally located the bag he'd been searching for and headed for the deck, where he cautiously approached the tail of the seven-foot-long reptile. "Barney is an old friend," he explained. "For all practical purposes, he should be holed up in his winter nest."

With his bare toe, Remy nudged the tip of the gator's tail, then quickly stepped backward. He heard Jane gasp, but ignored her and kept his eyes trained on Barney. "But every once in a while," he continued softly, "the old boy's sweet tooth starts bothering him."

"You've got to be kidding!" Jane exclaimed.

"Shh…" Remy shot her a quick warning glance. "Just stay still." Keeping a wary eye on the reptile, he pulled a couple of marshmallows out of the bag. The second he dropped one, the old gator turned, quick as a flash in a flurry of movement, and scrambled toward the lone marshmallow. Within the blink of an eye, the marshmallow disappeared inside the gator's powerful jaws.

"That's right, old boy," Remy crooned. "Come and get 'em." He dropped another marshmallow, then jumped backward as the gator scrambled after it.

It took three more marshmallows, but Remy was finally able to coax the big gator back into the water.

"You can come down now," he called out to Jane.

"I—I think I need some help."

Immediately assessing the problem, Remy strode over to the table, which had only three legs and wasn't built to hold much weight. The way she was balanced, one wrong move could topple her and the table.

"How the hell did you manage to get up there in the first place?" He lightly tapped her cast. "Especially with that thing?" When he had her firmly by the waist, she suddenly twisted and clung to him with her good arm. The feel of her breasts crushed against his chest and her hand clutching his bare shoulder as he swung her down sent sudden, unexpected shivers of desire coursing through him. When he released her, a flush stole over her cheeks and she wouldn't look him in the eyes, making him wonder if she'd experienced the same sensation he'd felt or if she was simply embarrassed.

"I'm not quite sure myself how I got up there," she said, her voice a bit strained. "But it was either the table or the water." She backed away and yanked on the tail of her shirt, which had bunched up at her waist. "Not much choice." She peered past him, a suspicious look on her face. "Are you sure your friend is gone?"

Remy nodded. "Yeah, I'm sure."

Jane walked the length of the deck and peeked over the rail. "How did he climb onto the deck?"

Remy scratched his head. "That's what I haven't quite figured out yet. And believe me, I've tried."

She gave him another suspicious look. "What are the chances of him coming back?"

He shrugged. "If it was summer, I'd say tomorrow, but since it's November, probably not for several days, if then."

She swallowed hard, and a delicate shiver made her shudder. "Coffee," she muttered. "I need a cup of coffee." Doing an about-face, she headed for the kitchen. "I had just put on a pot to brew," she continued, "and had stepped outside when that—that thing showed up." She paused inside at the kitchen counter to glance over at him. "I didn't mean to scream, but he startled me."

Remy suppressed a grin. "Barney has that effect on people," he said dryly.

She frowned. "Why the name Barney?"

Remy shrugged. "He's big and in the same family."

"Sorry, you lost me."

"You know—Barney, the big purple dinosaur character." She didn't know, he decided. There wasn't even a glimmer of recognition in the confused expression on her face. Didn't know or didn't remember. "Barney is a television character that's loved by every kid under three years old."

She stared up at him, her expression thoughtful yet troubled. "Do you think that means I don't have children? Surely if I did, I would know about this Barney character."

The wistfulness in her tone was almost Remy's undoing. He wanted to reach out, gather her close and hold her, somehow comfort her. Instead, he grabbed the coffeepot. "Not necessarily," he answered gruffly. He snagged a mug and filled it. "Not every parent is as enamored with Barney as his or her children.'' He handed her the mug, then filled one for himself.

The trouble was, he could picture her with children, especially a small, blond-haired girl with big brown eyes. And if a child existed, then it stood to reason there was a husband.

Remy tightened his grip on the coffee mug. Since he'd found his mystery lady on Willow Island, he'd run the gamut of scenarios about her in his mind, but none of them had included a child or a husband.

It was possible, so why hadn't he considered it?

*Maybe because you're falling for the woman and didn't want it to be true.*

The thought was like a hot knife slicing his insides.

Space, he decided. What he needed was some space, some time away from her to get his head on straight. And he needed to find out who the hell she was and who had tried to murder her. Anything else, most especially anything personal, would be the height of stupidity on his part...nothing but sheer foolishness.

# CHAPTER EIGHT

ON FRIDAY MORNING, Jane awoke to the sound of Remy cranking the motor on his boat. He was leaving…again, and with a sinking feeling, she listened as the loud noise began to fade with distance.

"Another day, just me and the mosquitoes," she grumbled, staring up at the whirling blades of the ceiling fan. Another day without even a glimmer of memory of who she was and where she'd come from. Being isolated on the houseboat might be the safest place for her, but without Remy's imposing presence, it was beginning to feel like solitary confinement.

She'd spent most of Thanksgiving by herself, except for the short time Remy had returned, loaded down with a basket full of every kind of food imaginable. He'd explained that the food was compliments of his aunt, a Goodwill package of sorts, designed to make him feel guilty for refusing to join the family for Thanksgiving dinner. Jane personally thought it was a strange way of trying to make someone feel guilty, and she worried that she was the reason he hadn't stayed.

When she'd voiced her concerns, Remy had simply shrugged them away. "I wouldn't have stayed, anyway," he'd said. "To put it mildly, some of my family don't exactly get along, and even though Aunt

Mary's house is sort of like a demilitarized zone for everyone, I try to avoid family gatherings.''

Jane turned on her side in the bed, drew her knees up to her stomach and pulled the sheet to her chin. The bitterness in his tone had been unmistakable, arousing her curiosity. She'd wanted to know more about him and what had happened in his past to make him such a loner, but his remote demeanor hadn't invited questions or conversation, and as soon as he'd cleared away the food and washed their dishes, he'd left again.

But curiosity wasn't all he aroused. Jane closed her eyes. A mistake. Lately it seemed that each time she closed her eyes, Remy filled her thoughts...the way tiny sun wrinkles radiated from the outside corners of his piercing emerald eyes...the scent of him, masculine, earthy....

She groaned. She wasn't sure at exactly what point she'd begun to fantasize about Remy Delacroix, but she had, and it was driving her to distraction. She still wasn't one-hundred-percent sure she trusted him. There were just too many unanswered questions about his involvement in the whole mess, so what she needed to do for now was concentrate on regaining her memory and finding out who she was.

Using the relaxing technique that Sam had suggested, Jane began to breathe deeply and exhale slowly. If she could just clear her mind....

When she next awoke, she felt disoriented and her heart was thudding beneath her breasts. Had she been dreaming or was the sound she'd heard real?

Then an icy finger of fear traced a path down her

spine as she heard the noise again: shuffling, sliding footsteps on the deck, just outside her window....

A scream lodged in her throat and she bit her lip to hold it back. Had the person who had assaulted her and left her for dead somehow discovered she was alive and traced her to the houseboat?

"Oh, God," she whispered as a tiny moan escaped her throat and, outside, the wooden deck creaked. The footsteps grew fainter, and she held her breath, hoping that whoever was out there would simply go away.

*It could be Remy,* a voice of reason tried to point out, just before she heard the groan of the back door opening.

No, not Remy, she thought frantically, as paralyzing terror seized her. Remy's steps were distinctive—firm and purposeful—and he had a habit of calling out her name before he even entered the house.

Besides, Remy had left. She'd heard him go. And now...now she was all alone, except for whoever was trying to get in the back door.

WHEN REMY REACHED the swamp-tour pier, Ray was pulling away from the dock with a boatload of noisy customers.

Remy gave the guide a brief salute, then glanced at his watch. For a change, Ray was right on schedule.

As Remy moored his boat, he reviewed the mental timetable he'd set for himself. He'd managed to leave the package of fingerprints for Charly with his aunt the day before without running into his father or brother. But the other person he'd hoped to see hadn't been there. His cousin Joanna had called ahead to say she was running late and had arranged for his sister, Toni, and another niece, Shelby, to take her place helping Mary.

He suddenly grimaced, remembering how Toni and Shelby had cornered him and tried to persuade him to stay and enjoy the family get-together. Remy would have liked nothing better, but as he'd explained to them, he doubted that anything short of selling his business and becoming an attorney would ease tensions enough for his father to relax and truly enjoy his company.

Remy headed toward the gift shop. Because there wasn't a whole lot more he could do about tracing Jane's identity before Monday, he'd decided to continue his investigation of the survey stakes, and since he hadn't been able to talk with Joanna on Thanksgiving, he hoped to track her down today.

Nodding to a tourist sitting on the small porch in front of the gift shop, Remy entered the building. He had a nagging feeling that Jane's presence and the stakes were somehow linked, especially since he'd found there was a good possibility she was connected with the Department of Environmental Standards.

After a brief search inside, Remy finally located Claudia out back, where they kept the live fishing bait. She wasn't alone. Her customer, a dark-haired, ragtag boy who looked to be about twelve, was holding a cane fishing pole with one hand and digging in his pockets with his other one.

Claudia gave Remy a brief nod of acknowledgment, then returned her attention to the boy

"Worms, crawdads, shrimp or minnows?" she asked.

"Which is the cheapest? I've only got—" the boy pulled his hand out of his pocket and counted the handful of change "—fifty cents."

Claudia studied the boy for a minute, then turned to the wooden box where they kept worms. She reached inside with her bare hand, stirred the dark loam, then produced a handful of fat, wriggling worms. "These'd be your best bet for the money," she said.

The boys eyes widened. "Wow, those are a lot bigger than the ones I dug up."

Remy left them to it. A few minutes later, seated at his desk in the office, he tapped out his cousin's home phone number. There was no answer.

He depressed the switch and punched out the phone number to his father's law office. Maybe Joanna was at work. Three rings later, the answering machine clicked on and Remy hung up the phone.

He was checking the past week's receipts when Claudia came to the office door. He glanced up. "I take it your customer left," he said.

"I know, I know!" Claudia rolled her eyes toward the ceiling. "He didn't have enough money. But today's his *grand-mère*'s birthday. Seems she's got a real hankering for fish, and since he ain't got enough money to take her out to eat, he figured he'd catch some and surprise her." She gave a little, one-shouldered shrug. "So, take it off my next paycheck."

Remy chuckled. "You're a soft touch, Claudia, and he knew it. Now, go wash your hands so you can bring me up to date on the accounts. And Claudia—''

She raised her eyebrows.

"Don't forget that smudge on your nose."

AN HOUR LATER, armed with the grocery list he'd made out earlier, Remy drove his truck toward downtown. He was a block away from the store when, at the last minute, he made a split-second decision and turned left onto the street where his father's law office was located.

Up ahead, he instantly recognized his cousin's distinctive 1959 midnight blue Mercedes sedan parked in the small driveway.

Remy pulled in alongside of the sedan and jumped out of his truck. He was halfway up the sidewalk when the entry door of the office opened and Joanna stepped out.

"Well, hello, stranger," she called, flashing him a smile as she locked the door to the office. She immediately stepped forward to give him a hug.

Remy returned her hug. His cousin had come back to Louisiana two years before, following her husband's death. Since then Remy had learned that they shared many things—a fierce independence, a strict sense of right and wrong, and the incomparable heartbreak of having lost a deep love.

Remy had also learned that Joanna was someone who would always give him a straight answer.

When she pulled away, she smiled up into his face. "I stopped by your office earlier this week to say hi. Claudia either didn't know where you were or seemed hesitant to say. Is everything okay?"

"Fine," Remy lied. "Just busy taking care of a few things. I wish I could say I just stopped by for that hug, but truth is I thought you might help me with something. I've found some survey stakes in the swamp on your dad's land. Know anything about them?"

Her eyebrows rose in genuine puzzlement. "Survey stakes on my father's land? Which part?"

"Just east of Desiree's home in the swamp."

"Old stakes or new ones?"

"New, as far as I can tell."

Joanna frowned thoughtfully. "Well, this is news to me, Remy. But I can tell you this. If they're on my father's land then you can be sure *he* knows they're there and why. But I can ask him if you want me to."

"He'd come a lot closer to telling you something like that than telling me."

Joanna shook her head. "I wouldn't count on that, Remy. Since I left his law firm last year, my father and I are hardly what you'd call close. However, like I said, I will ask him for you. Shall I leave word for you at the office if I find out anything?"

Remy smiled. "Thanks, Joanna."

"My pleasure." Joanna glanced quickly at her wristwatch. "Remy, I hate to run, but I'd best be getting home. The van from Nikki's school will be dropping her off any minute. And there are a few things I need to get straight with that young lady as soon as possible."

Remy saw a flicker of uneasiness in Joanna's eyes. He took a step toward her. "Is everything okay with you and Nikki?"

Her small laugh held no mirth. "Let's just say Nikki's going on seventeen and I'm going on a nervous breakdown."

"Can I help?"

She shook her head and put on a brave smile. "Don't be concerned. It's just the teenage years. Everything's fine. Really."

Remy didn't believe Joanna for a minute. He had questioned and interrogated too many people over the years to be fooled by the front she was putting on for his benefit.

But he also knew that like him, his cousin guarded her privacy and found it hard to speak of her feelings. He would not trespass into an area that was obviously very sensitive.

They waved goodbye and he watched his cousin hurry to her car. As she drove away, the feeling that something was amiss between Joanna and her daughter grew even stronger. Under normal circumstance, the first question his cousin would have asked was why he was so concerned about the markers. The fact that she hadn't asked was a good indication of the extent of her distraction.

WHEN REMY PULLED HIS BOAT alongside the houseboat dock, a strange apprehension rippled through him. It was nothing he could put his finger on, but something seemed wrong…very wrong.

Inside, the house was quiet, and at first he figured that Jane was probably napping. But when he glanced around the kitchen, the uneasy feeling grew. The automatic coffeepot had shut itself off, but it was still half-full, just as he'd left it earlier, and other than his own empty cup, there were no breakfast dishes in the sink.

Within seconds he was standing at the bedroom door, staring at the empty, unmade bed. Jane's nightgown was lying in a heap on the pillow.

"Jane!"

He listened for a moment, but the only sound he heard was his own pulse beating in his ears. He quickly checked the bathroom but found it empty.

Cursing, he slammed his palm against the door frame. He shouldn't have left her alone. With a broken arm, she was helpless against…against…

*Think, man! Think! Don't jump to conclusions without all of the evidence.*

Remy carefully, methodically searched the houseboat. Everything seemed just as he'd left it, and there was no sign of a struggle. Finding nothing amiss, he stood in the middle of the living room, drew in a deep gulp of air, then released it in a sigh.

There was only one place left to check. With heavy steps, Remy returned to the deck. Squinting against the bright sunlight, he moved slowly along the rail and searched the brackish water that surrounded the houseboat. Scenes of floating, bloated bodies found in the canals and waterways around New Orleans flashed through his mind. In his years as a detective, there had been more than he cared to count.

But there was no body this time. Thank God.

*Now what?* Remy shoved his fingers through his hair and stared into the distance. Where could she have gone? But more to the point, had she gone willingly? And where the hell did he even start to look?

The noise was faint at first, but Remy instantly recognized it as the sound of an outboard motor approaching. As it grew louder, he walked to the front corner of the porch near the pier. When a small skiff came into sight from behind a stand of cottonwoods, he recognized it immediately as Desiree's. But the old woman wasn't alone.

Jane was with her.

Relief warred with simmering anger, and the simmering anger built to the boiling point, so that by the time the skiff pulled alongside the pier, Remy saw nothing but a red haze of fury. And in the center of that fury was Jane.

THE SMILE OF GREETING on Jane's lips faded the moment she sighted Remy.

"Where the hell have you been?" he demanded, glaring down at her.

Jane was stunned, too stunned to answer him at first.

"I brought you here to keep you safe, not for you to run all over the bayou." He snatched up the rope Desiree held out and secured the boat to the pier. "Don't you think that the least you could have done was leave a note?" Each word was a sarcastic barb, and like a flash of lightning, Jane's own temper suddenly flared.

She narrowed her eyes and gritted her teeth. How dare he talk to her as if she were a rebellious teenager? Then she felt Desiree's hand pat her clenched fist.

The old woman laughed. "Don't pay no never mind to Remy, child," the old woman said. "He gets all riled up when things don't go his way, but he'll get over it."

Still trying to keep a lid on her simmering temper, Jane pointedly ignored Remy's outstretched hand and climbed out of the boat. If anyone knew him, it was Desiree, and maybe he hadn't meant to be so nasty. Maybe his bark was worse than his bite. Still...

Jane whirled to face him on the dock. "To answer your first question," she retorted, "Desiree invited me along on her rounds this morning."

"Invited" wasn't exactly how it had happened, but close enough. The old woman had just about scared her spitless when she'd come shuffling along the deck.

"And to answer your second question," Jane continued, sarcasm dripping with each word, "it never entered my mind that I had to get permission or sign in and sign out, like some kind of prisoner."

For what seemed like an eternity, she and Remy stared at each other, and the heavy, humid air seemed to crackle with undercurrents of tension.

Then Remy abruptly turned away to help Desiree out of the boat, and the spell was broken. "Next time leave a note," he snapped before stalking off. When the kitchen door slammed soundly behind him, both Jane and Desiree flinched.

Again Desiree laughed. "Just as I figured. The first time I laid eyes on you, I knew you were perfect for him. And I was right. He's only mad because he's taken a shine to you."

Sudden heat burned Jane's cheeks. "That's ridiculous," she muttered, still staring at the closed kitchen door.

"Not so," the old woman retorted. "It's been a long time for him since his Julie was killed, and he's ripe and ready. And of course it helps that you've taken a shine to him, too."

Jane whirled to face the old woman, a ready denial on the tip of her tongue. But the knowing expression on Desiree's face and the hypnotic, unnerving gleam in her faded eyes kept Jane silent.

*I feel as if I should know you, or that we've met before....*

Her own words came back to haunt her, and for a moment Jane felt disoriented and dizzy. But Desiree had said that they had never met before.

Jane closed her eyes and breathed deeply, and when she opened them again, the unsettled feeling had passed.

"Who was Julie?" she asked. "His wife?"

"Not his wife, his woman." Jane wanted to know more, but even as she open her mouth to ask, Desiree shook her head. "If you want to know more about Julie, you'll have to ask Remy. More is not for me to say." The old woman turned away. "I think we could all use a cup of tea, and then I need to be on my way. I'm almost out of willow bark, and I wanted to scout out a large grove of black willows that Flora said a friend of hers spotted over near..."

Desiree's words faded in and out as Jane followed her into the kitchen and sat down at the table. She tried concentrating on what the old woman was telling her, something about brewing willow bark into a tea that was good for arthritis. But all she could think about was what Desiree had said earlier out on the dock.

Hunching forward, Jane planted her elbows on the table and supported her forehead with the heel of her hand. Was Desiree right? Had Remy "taken a shine" to her? And worse, had she to him? And what about the mysterious Julie, the woman Remy had once cared about so much that he'd kept to himself ever since her death?

Jane pressed her head harder, as if the pressure could push the confusing thoughts out of her mind. None of it mattered, anyway. Until her memory returned, until she found out who she was, everything else was irrelevant.

She jumped when she felt Desiree's bony hand on her shoulder. "Has your *mal de tête* returned?"

Jane sat up straight. "My what?"

"Your headache? It has returned?"

Jane shook her head. "No…not exactly. I guess I'm just tired."

"Hmm…" The old woman nodded. "Well, drink this." She placed a steaming mug on the table. "It will help you feel better. And stop worrying so much. Everything will work out like it's supposed to. It always does."

REMY DIDN'T JOIN THEM for tea, and after Desiree left, Jane retreated to the bedroom and took a nap. When she awoke, there was a note propped up against the lamp on her bedside table. Remy had written that he had left her a sandwich in the refrigerator and that he had decided to go fishing. In the last sentence, he'd scrawled that if she needed anything, all she had to do was yell, since he would be fishing nearby.

*If she needed anything...* She needed to regain her memory, she thought desperately, and just as important, she needed to know who had tried to kill her and why.

She pushed herself out of bed and made her way slowly to the kitchen. There, as promised, she found a turkey sandwich waiting in the refrigerator.

After she'd poured herself a glass of milk, she sat at the table and stared out of the window as she bit into the sandwich. She strongly suspected that Remy's fishing trip was designed to give each of them some much-needed space after their blowup. A part of her was relieved, but another part felt bereft and at loose ends.

She could always watch TV, she supposed, but reading held more appeal, and surprisingly enough, the day before she had discovered that Remy had quite a collection of books. Though most of them were heavy law tomes, she'd also found books on nature and wildlife as well as fiction.

By late afternoon Remy still hadn't returned. She'd long ago lost interest in the book she'd been reading, and with no one to talk to and nothing to do but think, she'd found her imagination beginning to get the best of her.

What if something happened to him? What if he didn't return? Then what would she do?

More than once she found herself staring at the telephone and wondering if she should call the police, after all. But each time she reached for the phone, she could hear Remy's warning. *If I were you, I wouldn't trust anyone....*

She was outside pacing the deck, trying to decide if she should do as his note had instructed and yell for him, when she heard the distinct sound of an outboard motor start up. With her good hand shading her eyes against the setting sun, she searched the surrounding marshlands.

The moment the boat appeared from behind a nearby stand of bald cypress, she did an abrupt about-face and stomped inside the houseboat.

Even though he'd said he wouldn't be far away, she hadn't realized just how close he actually was. The thought that he had probably been watching her all along and had more than likely seen her pacing the deck like a madwoman was infuriating and embarrassing.

Fishing, indeed, she thought as she snatched up the book she'd been reading and plopped down onto the sofa. More like spying, she thought as she stared at the pages of the book.

"Jane?"

"In the living room," she snapped.

Her ears traced the sound of his footsteps from the deck through the kitchen. Without looking up, she knew the precise moment he entered the living room.

"Is something wrong?"

She slapped the book shut and glared at him. The puzzled look on his face was the last straw. She threw the book down and jumped off the sofa. "Just what kind of game are you playing?" she demanded.

His expression turned wary. "What are you talking about?"

"Oh, please, spare me. You know exactly what I'm talking about."

His eyes narrowed and he stepped closer. "No, I'm afraid I don't," he said evenly. "Why don't you just calm down and tell me what's got you so upset?"

"Upset? Me? What on earth do I have to be upset about?" she retorted, sarcasm dripping from each word. "Here I am, stuck in the middle of nowhere. No memory, not a clue as to why someone wants me dead, and no way to get off this damned boat, while you...you *pretend* to go fishing."

In two steps he was face to face with her, his hands gripping her shoulders. "Stop it! Stop it right now."

His mere touch jolted her like she'd been struck by a bolt of lightning. It was both heaven and hell. In a split second, everything changed. It was as if the floor had shifted beneath their feet, and they both froze. She inhaled sharply, and his masculine, earthy scent filled her nostrils. The very air between them sizzled, and as she stared into his eyes, she saw a reflection of her own desires and needs staring back at her.

"No..." he groaned. "Yes...oh, God..." Like a hawk diving for its quarry, he swooped down and took her lips in a devastating, mind-numbing kiss that shook her clear to her soul. Her insides quivered, and she found herself pressing closer to him, eager to feel the strength of him against her.

His hands found their way to her buttocks, and he lifted her up until she felt his erection, hot and stiff against her belly. She clung to him with her one good arm, cursing the cast that was wedged between them, while he continued his assault on her mouth and her senses.

"I tried," he murmured against her lips. "God knows I tried to avoid this." Before she could think, before she could respond, he kissed her again, this time with such aching hunger that her heart felt as if it would melt.

He was the first to break away. Gasping for breath, he snagged her hand and tugged gently. "Jane..."

The mere whisper of her name on his lips did funny things to her insides, and as she stared into his emerald eyes, eyes that were dark with passion and hunger, a trembling thrill raced through her.

"Come to bed. It's what we both want," he said. "And it's what we both need."

She was tempted. Oh, how she was tempted. "No," she finally whispered. She shook her head. "I can't." She tried to pull her hand free, but his grip tightened and she groaned in frustration. "You were right. I want to... But don't you see?" She shook her head again. "Until I know who I am, I can't. It wouldn't be fair—to you or to me. I could be married. I could have children...."

He closed his eyes and sighed. When he opened them again, they glittered with defiance. "You weren't wearing a ring when I found you, and no one has filed a missing person's report."

She smiled sadly. "It doesn't matter. You and I both know there could be any number of explanations for that."

He grimaced. "Yeah, I know." He finally released his hold on her. "Bad idea, huh?"

"Not bad, just...untimely?"

"I guess I owe you an apology then, so..." He shrugged. "For what it's worth, I'm sorry."

He didn't sound sorry in the least, and Jane smiled. "Me, too," she said softly. *More than you know,* she added silently.

Remy stared at her for a moment more, then reached up and rubbed the back of his neck. "How do you feel about fresh fish for supper?"

"Fish?"

He chuckled. "Yeah, whether you believe it or not, I really did go fishing."

Jane felt a flush steal up her neck. "I'd love some fresh fish."

Remy grinned knowingly, then turned and picked up the book she'd dropped earlier. He glanced at the title, then handed it to her.

"I hope you're not starving. I've still got to clean them, so it might be a while before we eat."

Jane clutched the book to her chest. "I can wait."

He nodded, turned to leave, then hesitated. "By the way." He faced her again. "I've decided to check out Willow Island once more in the morning. When I found you, I was in a hurry to get you back here, so it's possible I could have missed something."

A fluttery sensation rippled through her midsection. "Could I come along? Maybe seeing the place might jog my memory."

Remy frowned. "Tell you what. If you're awake when I get ready to leave, you can come. If not, I'll take you later."

Once Remy had left the room, Jane stared at the empty doorway, her insides churning. Part of her welcomed the chance to return to the island, but another part dreaded going back. What if the trip proved to be a waste of time and energy and she remembered nothing? Or worse, what if returning did jog her memory and she found out she had terrible secrets in her past?

# CHAPTER NINE

THERE WAS A DAMP CHILL in the air that went clear to the bone. A cold front, heralded by rain, had pushed through during the night, leaving the swamp gray and dismal.

Remy secured his boat on the narrow beach of Willow Island and headed for the spot where he'd found Jane. Earlier that morning, when he'd checked on her, she'd been snuggled beneath the covers of his bed. From the way she'd been breathing, he'd suspected that she was playing possum. For whatever reason, he guessed that she'd changed her mind about going with him. He'd been tempted to speak to her, but decided that later in the day, when it was warmer, might be a better time for her to travel on the water.

Even though the rain had washed the ground clean, he found the spot he was looking for without any trouble. From that point Remy began his search by walking in ever-wider circles, closely examining each square foot of turf.

He'd been searching the area for twenty minutes when he finally spotted something that caught his interest. Sticking up out of the water in a small boggy area was a muddy object that appeared to be a strap of some kind. He squinted and his heart thumped beneath his rib cage. Since the bog was surrounded by tall swamp grass, the water surface covered in duckweed, he could have easily overlooked the object the day he'd found Jane.

Remy knew better than to step too close. Whole cows had been known to disappear in bogs like this.

Glancing around, he found a long fallen branch that was forked at one end. Hefting it in his hand, he hunkered down near the water's edge and began carefully probing, trying to hook the strap. Common sense told him it could be nothing, but when he finally snagged it and pulled, his pulse raced with anticipation. The strap was connected to a large, weighty tote bag.

Ever so carefully, Remy slowly pulled the bag toward him until it was close enough for him to grab with his hand. Once he'd secured the canvas object, he tried to unzip it, but the teeth of the zipper were caked in mud and had already begun to rust.

Cursing in frustration, Remy stood and withdrew his pocket knife. In seconds he'd ripped open the bag. He'd expected to see a soggy mess, but was surprised to find that the bag was waterproof. Inside, perfectly intact, were papers, cardboard tubes and a leather object at the very bottom that he suspected was a pocketbook.

Remy started to reach inside the bag but hesitated. His hands were filthy. Gripping his find firmly, he jogged back to where he'd moored his boat. There he rinsed his hands in the bayou and dried them on the tail of his shirt. Seated in his boat, he carefully examined the contents of the bag. The first thing he took out was the leather pocketbook, and the first thing he saw when he opened it was a Louisiana driver's license. His heart began to pound. The woman pictured on the license was Jane.... Remy grimaced. No, not Jane. Hear real name was J. Kendall Delaney—J.K.D., the initials she'd scribbled in the logbook when she'd rented the boat. *Wonder what the J stands for,* he thought as he noted that the home address listed was Government Street in Baton Rouge. When the sudden, whimsical thought occurred to him that it just might stand for Jane, Remy instantly dismissed the idea as being too much of a coincidence, too weird.

At first, all he could do was stare at the license as he ran his finger back and forth over the picture. ''Kendall...Kendall...Kendall...'' He whispered the name, as if doing so would somehow make it fit the woman he'd come to think of as Jane.

When Remy was finally able to pull his eyes away from the license, he spied a small stack of cards stuffed inside another pocket. Business cards. Not only was Jane's name Kendall Delaney, but according to the business card, she was assistant director of the Louisiana Department of Environmental Standards. Remy shook his head as a sinking feeling settled into a hard knot in the pit of his stomach.

Finally, with slow deliberation, he closed the pocketbook and set it aside. Next he withdrew one of the cardboard tubes, pried open the plastic cap and pulled out the contents—a roll of survey maps.

It didn't take him long to determine that the maps were of the swamp in Bayou Beltane, and the hard knot twisted in his gut. By the time he'd examined the remaining contents of the tote bag, it was blatantly evident to Remy that someone was getting ready to drain part of the swamp and build a housing project.

Remy closed his eyes and cursed. Since most of the bayou was Delacroix property, split between his father and his uncle upon his grandfather's death, that someone could only be one person—Philip. He was the only member of the family who wouldn't think twice about destroying precious habitat if he stood to gain financially.

Equally disturbing to Remy was the fact that, according to the papers he leafed through, the project seemed to hinge on Kendall Delaney's approval.

Like the deadly venom of a snake, dark fury boiled and spread in Remy as his hand tightened around the sheaf of papers. There were strict laws in Louisiana protecting the wetlands, and bribery was the only way a project like this could have gotten as far as it had. Just how much had Philip paid some bureaucrat to push his dirty little deal through? Remy wondered. And was Jane a part of it? Was she on the take, too?

*Or was she a victim?*

Someone had tried to murder her. Had that someone known she wouldn't approve of the project? Was that the reason she'd been left to die?

Remy shifted uncomfortably. There were other reasons she could have been targeted. He didn't want to think it, but it was also possible that Kendall Delaney *was* a part of the deal and had tried to hold out for more money.

If he followed that scenario to its natural conclusion, not only would he be accusing her of blackmail, but he would be accusing his uncle of attempted murder. Not that Remy could picture his seventy-nine-year-old uncle actually committing the crime himself, but from the years he'd spent on the police force, Remy had no doubt Philip Delacroix had the resources and connections to have such a deed expedited.

Remy crammed the papers and tubes back inside the bag. For a split second, he was tempted to toss it back into the bog where he'd found it. But the moment passed. Doing so wouldn't solve anything, wouldn't make the problem go away. At best, it would only delay the inevitable. Eventually Kendall Delaney's memory would return, or someone would report her missing.

Four years ago, Remy had fought city hall. He'd tried to prove that there was graft and corruption in the NOPD, all the way to the top. He'd even set a trap, hoping to snare the traitors who called themselves officers of the law. But there had been a leak, Julie had been murdered and he'd been labeled a troublemaker and a pariah.

He'd lost everything four years ago, but not this time, Remy vowed. This time, with hundreds of acres of natural habitat threatened, there was too much at stake. This time the crooked bastards, including his uncle, weren't going to get away with their dirty deal. Remy would go to the press if he had to.

*What about Jane?*

He grimaced. Jane Doe, with her beautiful brown eyes, didn't exist, Kendall Delaney did. And if the government employee was part of an undercover scheme, then she deserved what she got.

Once Remy had shoved his boat off the beach, he

grabbed the starter rope of the motor and yanked. When the engine roared to life, he gave the throttle a vicious twist until it was running wide open.

As the boat plowed through the water, Remy scarcely noticed the bitter morning air stinging his face. His thoughts were consumed with the acres and acres of wetlands, and the thousands of wild creatures that would be destroyed if this development project went through—all hinging on the approval of a woman he'd grown to care too much about in a few short days.

*Kendall...Jane...* Once he confronted her with what he'd found, would her memory return? And if it did, would she care about the impact her decision could have on Desiree, the swamp, its creatures, even his own livelihood? Or was she just as greedy as his uncle?

Back at the houseboat, Jane was nowhere in sight as Remy tied off his boat. He had taken only a few steps toward the kitchen door when he heard another boat approaching. The moment he recognized Desiree's skiff, he groaned. He'd eventually have to tell the old woman what he'd found, but he'd hoped to delay doing so until after he'd confronted Kendall Delaney with her identity.

Desiree's boat slid up beside the pier. "You look like the cat that swallowed the canary," Remy told the old woman as he dropped the tote bag, secured her boat to the dock and helped her step up onto the pier.

Today she was wearing a black, flowing cloak. A multicolored scarf, predominantly red, was wrapped around her head and matched the dress that peeped from beneath the cloak. "What brings you out so early on this cold morning?" he asked.

Desiree smiled mysteriously and rummaged through the oversize bag that was slung over her shoulder. "I have something to show you," she said as she pulled out an envelope, yellowed with age. "I was digging in an old trunk last night, looking for a recipe, but I found this, instead." She handed him the envelope. "I thought it had been destroyed during Hurricane Audrey or I would have showed it to you before now."

Remy had been a mere child when the massive storm had wreaked havoc along the Louisiana coastline, but he still had terrifying memories of the howling wind and the devastation it had caused in the hours it had raged.

Growing more curious by the second, Remy slipped a brittle piece of paper out of the envelope. It was dated 1921, and as he scanned the handwritten contents, his heart slowed to a dull thud. It was a signed deed made out to Desiree from his grandfather, Hamilton Delacroix, giving the old woman forty acres in the middle of the swamp.

Remy's pulse quickened. According to the deed, the forty acres in question sat smack dab in the middle of Delacroix land, the land clearly marked off by the survey he'd found in the bag belonging to Kendall Delaney.

"You couldn't have found this at a more opportune time," he said, impulsively hugging the old woman as he tried to contain the excitement racing through his veins. "This is exactly what we need."

Desiree smiled. "Of course."

Behind them, the kitchen door opened. "I just put on a fresh pot of coffee, if anyone is interested."

Remy slowly turned his head. Seeing Jane was a stark reminder of what he'd found on Willow Island. No, he thought. Not Jane. Her name was Kendall Delaney, and the faster he accepted that reality, the better.

"A cup of coffee to warm an old woman's bones is just what the doctor ordered." Desiree cackled and hurried toward the kitchen. "Come along, Remy," she called over her shoulder. "From the look on your face, I think you have something to tell us."

Muttering to himself about mind readers disguised as old women, Remy snatched up the muddy bag and trudged after Desiree. The news of her discovery had helped to take the edge off of his anger, and now all he felt was dread for the task before him.

WHEN REMY ENTERED the kitchen, Jane tried to appear calm. She shivered, but knew it was more from anticipation than from the damp, cool air that blew in the door with him.

While she was eager to learn if he'd found anything on Willow Island, just the sight of him had her pulse jumping and her hormones raging. He was wearing a blue-and-brown-plaid flannel shirt and faded jeans, clothes that shouldn't have been especially appealing, but on him somehow managed to seem extraordinarily sexy. He needed a shave and had a rugged, windblown look that appealed to her on a level she seemed to have no control over.

Once she'd handed out the steaming mugs of coffee, she seated herself opposite Desiree. It was then that she noticed the canvas bag Remy dumped on the floor next to the chair he sat in.

He glanced at her and she pointedly eyed the bag. At first he didn't respond, except to take a sip of coffee.

"Time to spit it out, Remy," Desiree said. "Say it and be done with it."

"Say what?" Jane asked.

Remy shot his old friend Desiree an exasperated look, then turned and leveled his gaze at Jane. As she eagerly wait for him to speak, she suddenly felt as if thousands of butterflies were fluttering in her stomach.

"I know who you are," he said evenly.

Jane froze and for long moments couldn't utter a sound. "Who am I?" she was finally able to whisper. "What is my name?"

Remy reached down beside his chair and pulled a wallet out of the tote bag. Jane held her breath as he opened it and placed it on the table in front of her. "Your name is Kendall," he said. "J. Kendall Delaney."

"Kendall Delaney," she whispered. Staring at the picture on the license, she kept repeating the name in her mind. At first it meant nothing.

Then, abruptly, a strange sensation came over her in a rush, so powerful and potent it took her breath away. *J. Kendall Delaney...Janet Kendall Delaney...* Her vision blurred and spots began to dance before her eyes as a barrage of jumbled memories assailed her like a thousand tiny darts, each making a direct, painful hit.

She must have moaned because she could hear

Remy calling her name, asking if she was okay. But the very next moment, the room grew darker and began to fade. She felt as if she was free-falling, tumbling through time and space. Then everything went black.

When Kendall came to, she was lying on the sofa with Remy seated on the edge next to her. Desiree hovered over her, patting her face with a cool, dampened dish towel.

There were still gaps in her memory, Kendall realized, but for the most part, she remembered everything...everything but the so-called accident or the person who had assaulted her.

She looked into Remy's eyes. There was concern, but also something else—a wary, almost distrustful look that puzzled her.

"How are you feeling?" he asked.

"I... Oh, Remy, I remember. I remember almost everything. My poor mother must be worried sick."

"Your mother?"

She nodded. "She's an invalid. Totally dependent on me. I—I was supposed to be gone for only a couple of days, and a family friend is staying with her until I get back. I have to get to the phone." She tried to rise, but Remy grabbed her shoulders and gently pushed her back down.

"Easy now," he said. "Just take it easy a minute. First things first. We know who you are now, but we still don't know who tried to murder you or why. Before I let you do anything, I want you to try and recall what happened the day I found you."

Kendall closed her eyes and sighed. She owed

Remy her life, and after all he'd done for her, the very least she could do was give him an explanation.

"Okay," she finally said, and when she tried to rise this time, he helped her up. She scooted to the end of the sofa and curled her feet beneath her.

"Why don't you start at the beginning," he suggested, crossing his arms over his chest. "Start with...say, the day you arrived. Where did you go and what did you do?"

Kendall stared at a wildlife painting hanging on the opposite wall, but instead of the painting, she saw herself standing before Don Talbot, her boss, the day he had assigned her to check out the survey.

Just the thought of the short, overweight man left a bad taste in her mouth. She'd long suspected that he was up to his eyeballs in graft and dirty deals, but there was no way she could prove it. She'd also suspected that he was using her to cover his own tracks when he'd given her the Bayou Beltane project. But again, she had no proof.

Kendall blinked, then sighed. She would tell Remy what he wanted to know, but there was no point in telling him everything, especially since doing so could mean losing her job.

She turned to Remy. "I work for the DES and was given an assignment, assigned to do an environmental impact assessment but you already know that. I arrived late Sunday afternoon and checked into the Beltane Motel. Even though the assignment would normally take a couple of days, I had hoped if I got an early start Monday, I could finish up and be home that evening, or early Tuesday at the latest."

"Why hasn't anyone come looking for you or reported you missing, especially the motel?"

She shrugged. "The motel has my credit card number, so why would they care, one way or the other? Payment for the room was guaranteed. And no one else except my mother would be worried, what with the Thanksgiving holidays and all." She shrugged again. "Anyway, there's really not much more to tell except that I do recall renting the boat and checking the stakes on Willow Island." She frowned. "But after that, everything's kind of cloudy. I'm sorry, but I don't remember anything else." She paused, and like a strobe light, flashes of other memories hit her.

"Except..." She turned to stare at Desiree, who had seated herself in a nearby chair. "When I entered the motel room, there was a voodoo doll lying in the middle of the bed." Kendall could feel her pulse racing. "I thought it was simply some kind of weird local custom, so I didn't pay it much attention, but now... Oh, my God...the doll—its arm was broken."

Desiree smiled sadly. "And you think I am responsible in some way, eh? Maybe you even think I'm the one who tried to harm you?"

Kendall didn't want to believe it, but even as she shook her head in denial, she knew the old woman was right. "I—I don't know what to believe. I just don't know."

"That's the most ridiculous thing I've ever heard." Remy jumped to his feet and glared down at her. "How can you even think such a thing after all that Desiree has done for you?"

"Now, Remy—" The old woman held up her hand in protest.

"No!" Remy shook his head. "I will not allow her to malign you like this."

Kendall felt like crawling under the sofa. While it was true that Desiree had been nothing but kind to her, what other explanation could there be? The old woman stood to lose a hell of a lot if Kendall's assessment proved favorable to the housing project, and Desiree was the only person she knew who practiced voodoo. But there was more to it than just the voodoo. There was that strange familiar feeling she'd had all along that she'd met Desiree before.

Intending to try to defend herself, Kendall glanced at Remy. A mistake, she decided. His expression had hardened, and his eyes were like slivers of green ice, cold and distant. She swallowed hard. There was only one thing left to do. "I think it would be better for everyone concerned if I returned to the motel. In fact, I insist on it."

"You're forgetting something. Despite what you think you know, Desiree isn't the one who tried to kill you. But someone did and that someone is still out there."

Kendall didn't know what to believe anymore, but one thing she did know. She was confused and she needed space to sort out her feelings. She pushed herself off the sofa and stood face-to-face with Remy. "Either you take me back to the motel or I'll call the police to come get me."

# CHAPTER TEN

PHILIP DELACROIX STARED at the preliminary PR literature his campaign manager had dropped off at *Belle Terre* for approval. He reached up and tugged at his bow tie, trying to ignore the nausea in the pit of his stomach and the worrisome ache in his left shoulder, which had started up again when he'd opened his front door earlier to find another one of Flora Boudreaux's evil gris-gris lying on the veranda. The damned woman was becoming a menace.

Philip cursed and shoved the papers to the far corner of his desk. How could he be expected to concentrate on a stupid campaign when he was feeling so lousy? Thinking about an election that was still almost a year away was the last thing he wanted to be bothered with. And he certainly didn't want to think about the young upstart who was bound and determined to unseat him as a state senator. On top of everything else he hadn't heard a word from that fool Don Talbot in days.

What's more, now he had to worry about Nikki seeing Steven Boudreaux!

What a mess, he thought as he reached for the drawer in his desk where he kept a bottle of antacids. Lately it seemed as if he were popping them like candy. Wouldn't surprise him at all if he had an ulcer. He certainly had enough provocation for one!

A car door slammed outside the library window. Philip looked out to see his daughter, Joanna, approaching the veranda. He glanced at his watch. Prompt as ever. The antacid would have to wait.

While most families had their black sheep, he had his own personal Judas in the form of Joanna. But blood was blood, and despite her defection to his brother's firm, she was still his daughter. And Nikki's mother.

Nikki! That bitter argument he'd had with his granddaughter the day before still burned in his ears. He had done his best to warn her away from Steven Boudreaux. But she refused to listen. Foolish, stubborn girl!

Philip stood, took a deep breath and mentally prepared himself to greet his daughter. Joanna entered the room, looking as elegant and confident as ever. Her smile was polite, not warm.

"Thank you for coming," Philip said, irritated at the formality that Joanna had forced onto their relationship. His eldest daughter was tough and had an iron will, traits he'd always admired until she'd begun to use them against him.

He motioned her to a seat. "Coffee? Tea?"

She shook her head and remained standing. "I really don't have much time. But I'm glad you told my secretary you wanted to see me today. I've been trying to get a hold of you—"

"Yes, yes," Philip cut her off. "I got your messages to call. But I wanted to see you in person, Joanna. I see you so seldom now."

Philip had deliberately put a note of reproach into his tone. He still felt the sting of her betrayal. And he wanted Joanna to feel it. She gave no evidence that she did. But in the year Joanna had worked for him, Philip had learned that her actions indicated her feelings more than her words.

She still drove the 1959 Mercedes sedan that Philip had given her mother the day Joanna was born. Philip knew there was only one reason she would do that. Joanna was holding on to the symbol of love that had once joined them all together. Beneath his daughter's facade of cool indifference, he sensed her love for him.

"The reason I've been calling you is because Remy asked me—" Joanna began.

Philip held up his hand. "Whatever my nephew wants, it can wait. We have a much more important matter to discuss. You must put a stop to Nikki dating Steven Boudreaux. I've tried talking to the girl but she won't listen. It's time you—"

"Hold on, Father. I am just as upset about this as you, believe me. I've been doing everything in my power to stop her from seeing Steven. I know all about the yelling match you two had yesterday. I could have told you it wouldn't work. I've already been there. Telling her not to see him just makes her more determined to do so."

Philip watched something that looked almost like grief passing through Joanna's eyes. It surprised him. This time he did not coat his words with reproach. "This wouldn't be happening if you and Nikki hadn't left *Belle Terre.* Come back home, Joanna. I can protect Nikki from Steven Boudreaux there."

"How? By bringing guards into your home to watch her?"

"If necessary."

"In three months Nikki will be seventeen. She's growing into a young woman. She needs guidance to make the right choices, not chains to keep her from making mistakes."

"Your guidance hasn't stopped her from going out with that bastard!"

When Joanna suddenly paled, Philip knew he'd scored a direct hit. For once in his life, he hadn't meant to.

He circled his desk to stand in front of his daughter and took hold of her shoulders. "Joanna, let me help you. Come back to *Belle Terre*. Come back to the firm. We'll take care of Nikki together."

She looked directly at him, her eyes full of a deep strength and a deep pain.

"You're forgetting why Nikki and I moved out of your home and I left your firm."

Philip dropped his hands from her shoulders and whirled away. "I am not forgetting! My own flesh and blood! My first born! Where is your family loyalty? You turned on me, Joanna."

"You turned on the law. I'm an attorney. I have sworn to uphold the law. When I found out what you were doing, I had no choice but to leave your firm. And your home. Do you really think I would ever bring Nikki back here to learn her moral code from you?"

Her softly spoken words had been laced with steel. And that was when Philip knew that no matter how much love Joanna might still feel for him, it would never be enough.

The knowledge brought an acrid bile into his throat and fed the anger that closed like a tight fist around his heart. "Get out! Go!"

Without a word, Joanna turned and left the room.

Philip's stomach turned even more sour, and he broke out into a cold sweat. He cursed and fumbled behind him for the arms of his chair, then collapsed. With trembling hands, he wrenched open the top drawer, grabbed a bottle of antacid tablets, twisted off the cap and placed one in his mouth.

Outside, a car door slammed, an engine roared to life and tires squealed on the pavement.

Philip chewed the tablet, and while he waited for the pill to take effect, he mopped his forehead with a handkerchief as he stared at the contents of the drawer. The oversize acorn stuffed with hair and bearing four holes in its shell was still exactly where he'd placed it earlier. Philip knew enough about voodoo to know that the acorn was a death gris-gris, but what he didn't know was the proper way to dispose of the evil thing without incurring the curse it bore. He also knew that he'd been accused of being overly superstitious at times, especially when it came to voodoo, but he didn't consider himself superstitious. He simply figured it was always better to be safe than sorry, to always hedge his bets. After all, he thought, all of those old clichés about black cats and walking under ladders weren't still around for no reason. And damn her worthless hide, Flora knew how he felt.

"Damn you, Flora," he whispered. "Damn you to hell." Wasn't it enough that she taunted him by leaving the wicked gris-gris everywhere? Now he had to worry if his granddaughter was having an affair with Etienne Boudreaux, the boy Flora claimed was Philip's illegitimate son.

ACROSS TOWN, with Remy following close behind her, Kendall approached the room she'd rented at the Beltane Motel. The boat trip to the mainland had been silent and tense, but she'd felt his anger and disapproval with every movement he'd made. Once they had docked, she'd headed straight for her rental car, still sitting in the customers' parking lot near the gift shop. He'd placed her tote bag, along with the clothes he'd bought her, in the back seat. He'd stood and watched while she cranked the engine, and only then had he spoken.

"I'll follow you and check out the motel" was all he'd said before heading for his truck.

At the motel room, she inserted the key and unlocked the door, but before she opened it, she turned to face Remy. "I guess I seem pretty ungrateful after all you've done."

For a moment, it seemed that he wasn't going to answer. "*Ungrateful* is a good word for it," he finally said, his tone as cold and unrelenting as the expression on his face. "And it pretty much describes your behavior. I've known Desiree all my life, and I've never heard of her raising a hand in anger or intentionally hurting someone. And in case you've forgotten, she's ninety-three years old. Even if she wanted to strike someone, she wouldn't have the strength."

Kendall was at a loss for words, so she simply

stared at him. She had thought about it, to the point that she felt sick with guilt over her accusations against the old woman. Desiree had done nothing to warrant such suspicions, but for the life of her, Kendall couldn't shake the feeling that she'd seen the old woman before, and she couldn't come up with any other explanation, at least none that made sense. She'd witnessed the old woman ministering to her so-called patients, and even at ninety-three, Desiree possessed an uncanny physical strength when she needed it.

But Kendall had learned that when it came to Desiree, Remy was blind. His loyalty to the old woman blotted out everything else. She wished she had more concrete evidence for her suspicions than just her fear, but she also realized that nothing she could say would ever convince Remy. Saying anything more, in fact, would only tear a larger gap in their tenuous relationship.

Remy's only response was an ever-so-slight tightening of his jaw. Not knowing what else to do, she pushed the door open and entered the musty room. Her open suitcase was still sitting on the luggage rack, and the oversize T-shirt that she slept in hung on a nearby chair, exactly where she'd left it just days before.

Remy followed her inside and dumped her tote bag and sack of clothes on the floor. Then her gaze fell on the bed.

Lying on top of the faded bedspread in the middle of the pillows was a doll, just as ugly and just as hideous as the one she'd found on the day she'd first arrived. And stuck in the middle of its chest was a long, wicked-looking hat pin.

Kendall gasped and felt the blood drain from her face, but all she could do was sputter and point.

Remy pushed past her and marched over to the bed. He snatched up the doll and held it out to her. "I suppose you're going to try and convince me that Desiree is responsible for this, too."

Kendall could barely breathe as fear, like an icy finger, traced a path down her spine. A part of her knew exactly what the pin represented, but another part wanted to deny it. "She's the only person I know who practices voodoo," she was finally able to whisper.

"And you know so many people who live here," he retorted, sarcasm oozing from each word. "For your information, there are others in Bayou Beltane who practice voodoo, too. Several others, including Desiree's daughter, Flora. In fact, the moment you mentioned a voodoo doll, the person who instantly came to my mind was Flora, because she, unlike her mother, is not a very nice person, to put it mildly."

"But Desiree is the one who could lose everything if I approve the survey and write a favorable assessment."

Remy shook his head. "Not quite the only one. In case it hasn't dawned on you yet, my whole livelihood and the jobs of each of my employees are tied up with that swamp. And there are others—hunters, fishermen, and weekenders who have houseboats moored throughout the bayou and swamp."

"And do all of you practice voodoo?"

Suddenly, with a growl of pure frustration, Remy

turned, drew back his arm and flung the doll against the opposite wall. It ricocheted off and bounced to the floor. "Damn you!" he shouted. Hands on his hips, he glared at her. "Why do you have to be so stubborn about this? That old woman wouldn't harm a fly. But there's one thing I think we both can agree on. Someone out there is out to get you." Like the doll, his words seemed to ricochet off the walls. "Come back to the houseboat with me," he said at last, calming himself with an effort. "Just until I can get to the bottom of this. I can protect you there. Here..." He held out his arms in a helpless gesture. "I don't know."

"Why, Remy? Why does it matter to you what I do?"

To his credit, he didn't pretend to misunderstand her question. "Because, right or wrong, and as crazy as it seems, I care about you, dammit. More than I have about any woman for a very long time. It's as simple and as complex as that. I care."

From the dark, tortured look in his eyes, Kendall could see what the admission had cost him. He was a proud man, a man who didn't admit such things lightly, a man who had obviously been hurt deeply, so much so that, by his own admission, he hadn't had a relationship since the woman he'd loved had died, years ago.

Kendall wanted to go to him, wrap her arms around him, comfort him. And above all, she wanted to admit just how much she had grown to care about him, more deeply than she would have believed possible considering the short time they had known each other.

Yes, it was bizarre, and no, there was no rhyme nor reason as to how she could feel so strongly about a man she'd known for mere days. But she did...for all the good it would do her, since their relationship wasn't the only issue.

There were her suspicions about Desiree to consider. Going back with Remy would be admitting that she'd been wrong about the old woman, and regardless of what he'd said, regardless of what Kendall wanted to believe, she wasn't quite convinced of Desiree's innocence.

But even more than her suspicions, more than her fear for her own safety, she and Remy had a conflict of interest that was impossible to resolve. It was an issue bigger than both of them, something that neither could ignore or pretend didn't exist. She only hoped she could explain it without hurting him more than he'd already been hurt, because she was in torment enough for the both of them.

"Please try to understand," she said softly, imploringly. "Growing up, all I ever dreamed of was becoming an architect and of traveling the world to study the buildings of different cultures. My father sacrificed everything for me to get an education at the best university. He used up his savings and even let his life insurance policy lapse for my expenses. And when he died, there was nothing left...all because of me, because of my selfish dream."

Even now, the guilt still weighed heavily on her conscience, and though she'd told herself over and over that her father's financial decisions hadn't been entirely her fault, it was still hard to deal with.

"I had no choice but to drop out of school," she

continued. "And my mother has no one else but me now. She depends on me. And until I got this job, for years we were robbing Peter to pay Paul each month, living a hand-to-mouth existence."

Kendall raised her chin and looked Remy straight in the eyes. "I came here to do a job. And that job conflicts with everything you believe in and love." She shook her head. "It just wouldn't work. I can't go with you," she whispered. "Even if I wanted to."

"What if you found out that your job was an exercise in futility, that in the long run, your findings won't matter?"

She frowned. "I don't understand."

"Earlier, Desiree showed me a handwritten deed given to her by my grandfather. Unless I'm mistaken, it's a deed to the land that's been surveyed, land slated to be drained and turned into a big, exclusive subdivision, if your findings are favorable. I strongly suspect that my uncle is behind this whole thing, but once he finds out about the deed—and believe me, I intend for him to find out—then there's nothing he can do, and the assessment of environmental impact won't be worth the paper it's printed on."

Kendall tried to digest everything Remy had said, and though her heart ached, there was still only one possible conclusion. "I understand what you're telling me," she said. "But don't you see? None of that has anything to do with me. I was sent here to do a job, and whether you agree with it or not, or whether it's relevant or not, I still have to do it if I want to keep getting a paycheck."

Remy straightened to his full height, and the look he gave her seared her to the marrow of her bones.

It was a look of disbelief mingled with frustration, anger and pride, and it seemed to last an eternity. Then he turned abruptly and stalked past her. He grabbed the edge of the open door on his way out, and when he slammed it behind him, the whole room seemed to shake with the force.

Kendall winced, and for long moments, she simply stood there, staring at the closed door. Her eyes stung with unshed tears, and she wanted to run after him, tell him she would go with him or beg him to stay, anything to keep him with her. But she didn't... couldn't....

Why did life have to be so complicated? she wondered. So damned unfair and cruel?

*Remy is gone,* an inner voice taunted. *Gone for good, and the sooner you get that through your head, the better.*

And when all was said and done, the only person she could count on was herself.

Finally, she turned away, and with her eyes narrowed and her lips stretched into a thin line of determination, she walked over to where the voodoo doll lay. After only a moment's hesitation, she bent down and grabbed the evil object. Wedging it between her cast and her body, she took firm hold of the hat pin and jerked it out of the doll. Dropping both doll and pin in the trash can, she brushed her hands together as if dusting something vile from them, then walked to the door and hooked the safety chain.

Somewhere out there someone wanted her dead, but who? Desiree? Everything within Kendall shouted no. Then what about the old woman's daughter, Flora? Remy had insinuated she was a much more likely suspect than Desiree. And though Kendall couldn't recall ever meeting the woman, she couldn't completely dismiss her as a possible suspect. He'd also pointed out that any one of his employees would have a vested interest in keeping her from approving the development, since their livelihood depended on the swamp.

*And what about Remy?*

Kendall closed her eyes, and while a voice within her whispered that there was no way he could be responsible, she had to admit that her feelings for him could easily blind her to the facts.

Kendall groaned with frustration. If only *all* of her memory had returned. If only there weren't still gaps, then she might have the answers she needed. She might know who was out to get her.

With a sigh, she walked to the telephone. Sam had said she should eventually recall everything, and until then, all she could do was wait. Meanwhile she still had responsibilities.

She picked up the receiver and tapped out her mother's phone number. Doris Jones, the woman who was staying with her mother and a long-time family friend, answered on the second ring.

"Kendall? Oh, thank God! Your mother has been so worried about you."

"How is she, other than being worried?"

"Not good, I'm afraid. She hasn't been eating, and she's not sleeping at night. But what on earth happened to you? We've called and called, but—"

"Doris, it's a long story. Why don't you get Mom on the extension and I'll tell you both all about it."

Within seconds, Kendall heard the click indicating that her mother had picked up the extension.

"Kendall? Oh, honey, where have you been? I didn't know what to do or who to call."

It was a jolt to hear just how weak her mother's voice sounded. "Mom, it's okay. Just calm down. I'm fine. There were some problems here, some unexpected complications, and I had a little accident—"

"Accident! Oh, dear, are you hurt?"

"I fell and broke my arm, but I'm just fine. I promise."

"Not your left one again, I hope."

"No, Mom. It was my right one this time, and before you get started, no, I wasn't climbing a tree."

"Well, it wouldn't surprise me one bit if you were. You always were such a tomboy growing up—still are, for that matter. I'll never forget that other time you broke your arm. And then there was that time that you—"

"What's this I hear about you not eating?" Kendall interrupted, knowing that once her mother got started on her exploits as a child, she could go on and on.

By the time they finally hung up long minutes later, Kendall felt confident that she'd been able to set her mother's mind to rest. And she was almost sure that her mother's appetite would improve and she'd be able to rest better at night now that she knew Kendall was okay.

The next call she tried to make was to Don Talbot, but she got a prerecorded message and replaced the receiver. It had completely slipped her mind that today was Saturday and the office was closed.

With a sigh of frustration, she rummaged through her billfold and finally found the business card that had her boss's home phone number written on it.

Her call was answered on the second ring.

"Well, it's about time you checked in." Don Talbot coughed, then cleared his throat, and Kendall grimaced. "And I hope you called your mother. I've been out with the flu, and my secretary tells me there's a stack of messages waiting for me from the poor woman. I was just about ready to call the sheriff down there."

"I'm really sorry, Don, but I had a little problem." She repeated the story she'd told her mother about having an accident. And once again, she left out the part about her amnesia and the attempt on her life. "I'm going to need some more time on the project, I'm afraid."

"Hey, sweetheart, no problem."

Kendall shuddered at her boss's careless use of the endearment. She supposed she should be used to his chauvinism by now, but like everything else about the man, it still grated on her nerves.

"It's important to get this thing pushed through as soon as possible," he continued. "You know, pressure from the powers that be, jobs on the line—that sort of crap. But hey, stuff happens, so take a couple more days. We want to make sure it's done right or we'll have all those bleeding-heart environmentalists demanding our hides. Just make sure you come up with the *right* findings in that assessment, if you get my drift."

When Kendall hung up the receiver, she tried to swallow the bad taste that the conversation had left in her mouth. She'd worked for Don long enough to read between the lines. She could take her time, but she damn well better put her stamp of approval on the survey, regardless. He was using her. She was his sacrificial lamb in case of repercussions, someone to take the fall instead of him. And more than likely, just as Remy suspected, Don was probably getting paid by Remy's uncle to push the housing project through.

Kendall didn't like the idea that she was being used for less-than-ethical purposes. For a moment, she actually fantasized about out-and-out rejecting the development, for Desiree's sake as well as Remy's, but also for the sheer pleasure of watching Don Talbot squirm.

But the fantasy lasted only a moment before common sense and reality intruded. There was no way of proving that Talbot was using her, and she'd barely touched the tip of the iceberg when she'd told Remy about her financial situation and her responsibilities to provide for her mother. Until she'd been promoted to work under Don Talbot, there had been days when she'd counted pennies just to buy a loaf of bread. Without her job, there was no way she could afford the mounting doctor bills, the medications her mother needed or even the mortgage payment on the house.

EXHAUSTED, MENTALLY and physically, Kendall went to bed early that night. She wasn't sure how she would manage yet with her broken arm, but first thing in the morning, she intended to look into ways she could complete the job she'd come to do, even if she had to hire someone to take her back out to Willow Island.

But she soon discovered that going to bed early didn't guarantee going to sleep, and for what seemed like hours, she tossed and turned.

Unlike the soothing night sounds of the swamp, with its wind in the trees, lapping water and occasional far-off hooting of a barred owl, the noise of civilization intruded. Cars zoomed by on the highway. A police siren warbled in the distance. A stray cat yowled.

Then another noise intruded, from just outside her door—a scratching sound that didn't belong. And except for her heart pounding in her chest, Kendall went as still as death. Praying that she was mistaken, she dared not breathe as she strained her ears in the pitch-dark room. All she could think of was that she should have listened to Remy. She should have returned to the houseboat with him.

It was the sound of the doorknob turning that finally shook her out of her terrified stupor. She quickly scooted to the edge of the bed. Hoping to startle the intruder away, she flicked on the bedside lamp. But the doorknob jiggled again, and she belatedly realized that the windows must be covered with thick drapes.

"Go away!" Kendall screamed as she grabbed the telephone receiver. "I'm calling the police!" And with trembling fingers, she pressed 911.

Just as her call was answered, there was a loud thud against the door.

"I need help!" she cried into the phone, her voice shrill with terror. "Someone is trying to break into my room. Please help me! I'm at the Beltane Motel—room 121."

Another blow hit the door, hard enough to rattle the night chain.

Clutching the receiver to her ear, she didn't dare take her eyes off the door. Any minute, the flimsy lock was going to give and the intruder would burst into her room.

Instinct told her to run, to hide, to at least find something to defend herself with. But there was nowhere to go, no weapons to be had, especially for a woman with her arm in a cast.

All she could do was wait in horror while the person on the phone kept trying to reassure her that help was on the way.

# CHAPTER ELEVEN

AGONIZING SECONDS ticked by and turned into minutes. With one ear Kendall listened to the reassuring voice on the phone, telling her to keep calm, telling her not to hang up. With her other ear, she strained, listening for the slightest sound.

Strange, she thought. Now there was nothing but silence. Had the intruder finally fled?

Suddenly, the distant wail of police sirens broke the silence. The closer they came, the louder they grew. Then the sound of the sirens abruptly died, and it took Kendall a moment to comprehend what the voice on the telephone was saying.

"Ms. Delaney, the sheriff just radioed that he's in the motel parking lot and he's approaching the door. You can hang up and let him in."

"Thank you," she whispered, and before she could hang up the receiver, there was a sharp rap on the door.

"Ms. Delaney, this is Sheriff Trahan here. Are you okay?"

Kendall hung up the receiver and tried to answer, but the sound that came out was little more than a raspy croak. On rubbery legs, she made her way to the door. Her hand was shaking so hard she had trouble releasing the security chain. She could hear muffled voices outside, though she couldn't understand what they were saying.

Then one voice came through loud and clear. "Kendall, honey. Come on, open the door."

Kendall paused and her pulse skipped a beat. Unlike the first voice this one sounded achingly familiar. But Remy was angry with her. He had left, was probably back on the houseboat, sound asleep. Surely her mind was playing tricks on her, she decided, fumbling with the chain.

The first face she saw when she finally swung open the door was Remy's. Behind him, red-and-blue lights from the squad cars swirled in the darkness, silhouetting several men in uniforms.

"Are you okay?"

"Yes...no! Oh, God," she cried. "I don't know." And she flung herself into his arms.

He held her close, and though he was breathing hard, as if he'd been running, she was too overwrought to wonder why or do anything but seek comfort from the reassuring solidity of his broad chest and strong arms. His familiar, earthy scent engulfed her and she breathed deeply, drawing solace.

"I—I should have listened to you," she whispered, her voice little more than a squeak.

"You're okay now," he murmured. "He's gone and you're safe."

Kendall jerked away and stared up at Remy. "Gone? You mean they didn't catch him?"

Remy shook his head, and it was only then that she noticed the trickle of blood at the corner of his mouth. She reached up and gingerly touched his lip. "What happened to you?"

"It's nothing," he said gruffly, pulling back from her touch.

One of the uniformed men separated himself from the group and approached them. "Ms. Delaney? Sorry to interrupt, ma'am, but I need to ask you some questions."

Kendall didn't want to answer questions. She wanted to know why Remy was bleeding, why he was still breathing so heavily, but most of all, why he suddenly looked so miserable and ill-at-ease.

"Remy, why—"

He shook his head. "Not now, Kendall. Here, you're shivering." With one last squeeze, he released her, slipped off his jacket and placed it and his arm firmly around her shoulders. He turned them both to face the officer.

Kendall clutched the lapels together. The jacket was still warm from Remy's body heat, and until he'd given it to her, she's been so caught up her fear she'd completely forgotten that all she was wearing was the oversize T-shirt.

"This is Sheriff Jake Trahan. Sheriff, Kendall Delaney. You should feel honored," Remy told her, a trace of sarcasm in his tone. "Normally the sheriff doesn't lower himself to answer these kinds of calls personally."

Jake Trahan was a tall man with dark brown hair and green eyes. He had a confident air about him that inspired both trust and respect, and though most men would have been cowed by the daunting look in his eyes, Remy glared right back at him, almost defiantly.

"I live nearby," the sheriff said evenly, his gaze

still locked with Remy's. "I happened to be on my way home, but contrary to your obvious opinion, I care a great deal about what goes on in my hometown." After a moment more, he finally ended the silent standoff and turned to Kendall. Immediately, the look in his eyes grew warmer, more sympathetic.

"Why don't you tell me what happened?"

"There's not a whole lot to tell except that I heard a noise at the door and realized someone was trying to break in."

The chief nodded thoughtfully. Abruptly, he turned to Remy. "I know you used to be a hotshot detective with the NOPD, but this isn't New Orleans. You should have called in first before going off half-cocked and tackling that guy without backup."

"Yeah, right," Remy snapped. "What was I supposed to do, stand by and twiddle my thumbs while the creep waltzed right in?"

Comprehension suddenly dawned on Kendall. Remy had been there all along, had been sitting in the parking lot waiting and watching. She stared up at him, but his gaze never left the sheriff, and the only response he gave was the slight tightening of his arm around her shoulder.

Jake Trahan grimaced. "Okay, okay, you've got a point...but just remember, you're not the law. So why don't you help us catch this guy by telling me how it went down?"

Remy narrowed his eyes, and for a moment, Kendall thought he was going to refuse to answer.

REMY DEBATED the pros and cons of answering Jake Trahan. It still unnerved him every time he thought about how close he'd come to throwing in the towel after Kendall's declaration about her job earlier. He'd been so damned angry that he'd almost said to hell with it, had almost walked away.

*Yeah, and a lot of good it did her for you to stay. Some bodyguard you turned out to be.*

Remy gritted his teeth. The guy had thrown a lucky punch and had gotten away, and though Remy still wasn't sure if he'd have done anything differently, Jake Trahan was right. He should have tried to call for backup before tackling the bastard.

*And what about next time he comes after her?* Remy wanted to ignore the nagging voice that seared his conscience, but he couldn't. Had Sam been right? Was he being pigheaded and arrogant to think he could solve this thing on his own without any help?

He stared at the sheriff. Could he trust Jake Trahan? *Jake Trahan isn't like those others.* Desiree's words swirled inside his head. *You can trust him. Jake is a good man, an honorable man.*

Remy drew in a deep breath, and to his own amazement, he heard himself recounting everything, starting with the day he'd found Kendall, and only leaving out his suspicions about his uncle's connection with the survey. While he didn't much care for his uncle, he'd come to the conclusion that Philip would be the last person who would want to harm Kendall, especially since she seemed to have no choice but to approve the survey if she wanted to keep her job.

As Remy talked, a funny thing began happening. Little by little, the heavy weight of emotional baggage he'd been carrying around for the past four years began to lighten. And when he'd finished, for the first time since he'd moved back to Bayou Beltane he felt as if he was almost free.

"So what I guess I need from you is help," he said bluntly.

Jake Trahan's expression never changed. "You've got it," he answered. "And I'll go you one better. You keep me informed with whatever you dig up, and I'll do the same. You have my word on it, and maybe between the two of us, we can catch this guy." He pulled a pen and a small notebook out of his pocket. "Now, how about a description?"

Remy nodded. "He was wearing black jeans, black work boots and a black turtleneck sweater. He was also wearing a black-and-red ski mask, so I didn't get a look at his face. There's not a whole hell of a lot else to go on, but he was shorter than me—about five foot ten or so. And I guess he weighed about a hundred and sixty, but he was wiry and strong. Not the kind who pumps weights, but the kind who's used to physical labor." Remy shrugged. "I think his eyes were dark, probably brown, but I was kind of busy and didn't get a real good look. If he hadn't landed a lucky punch..."

"Not much to go on," Jake commented with a shake of his head. "But I'd be willing to bet he's a local. Otherwise he couldn't have disappeared so fast."

Remy nodded. "I suspect you're right, and to be honest, there was something familiar about him. I just can't put my finger on it yet."

"Well, if and when you do—"

"I'll let you know," Remy finished.

Jake turned to Kendall. "Ma'am, is there anything you can add to what Remy's said? Anything else you might have heard?"

Kendall thought back, trying to concentrate. "No," she finally murmured, shaking her head. "Nothing else."

"Well, if you do think of anything, let me know. Now…" He slipped the notebook and pen back inside his shirt pocket. "Would you like for me to have the management give you another room, in case your intruder comes back?"

Before she could answer, Remy interrupted. "I'll take care of it. It's too late to leave tonight, but for the record, first thing tomorrow morning she's coming home with me."

Jake raised an inquiring eyebrow aimed in Kendall's direction. Caught up in indecision, she hesitated, but all of the reasons she shouldn't go with Remy paled against the alternative of wondering when and where the man might try to get at her again.

She finally nodded. "You can get in touch with me there if you need me."

BY THE TIME REMY roused the management and secured another room, it was well past midnight and Kendall was exhausted.

"There are two beds," he said as he latched the night chain, then wedged a straight-backed chair beneath the doorknob. "I'll take the one nearest the door and you can have the other one."

Kendall didn't need to be told twice. She slipped

off his jacket, handed it over, then crawled into bed and pulled the covers up to her chin.

Remy went to the window, pulled back the edge of the curtain and stared out into the darkness. "There's a patrol car parked outside, so I don't think we have to worry about him coming back tonight." He dropped the curtain, then reached over and flipped the light switch.

The room was instantly plunged into darkness. Just the thought of the nameless man returning set off a bout of shivers, and Kendall curled into a ball beneath the covers, suddenly colder than she ever remembered being in her life.

She could hear the rustling of clothes as Remy undressed. When she heard the rasp of his jeans zipper, suddenly she could barely breathe. All that separated them was a scant two feet.

All of her adult life, she'd had to be sensible, had to be responsible. Just once, she wished she had courage enough to throw caution to the wind, to take what she wanted without having to consider the consequences. And now, at this moment in time, what she wanted more than anything was to feel Remy's comforting arms around her, to have the reassurance of his body close to hers.

She felt tears slide down her cheeks, and though reason said she was simply having a delayed reaction, she couldn't seem to stop shivering.

She sniffed and tried to muffle the distressed sounds that came unbidden from her throat.

"Kendall? Are you okay?"

"I—I'm f-fine," she whispered, hating herself for losing control.

"Oh, honey, don't." Within seconds, she felt the bed sink beside her and Remy's hand on her shoulder. "God, you're shivering. Come here, sweetheart." He gathered her, bedcovers and all, in his arms and held her close, crooning soothing words of comfort.

Kendall blindly reached out with her good arm and clung to him. Long minutes passed before she finally stopped shivering.

"All better now?"

She nodded against his shoulder. She was no longer afraid, but at some point, her need for comfort had turned into another kind of need, the need to feel his lips on hers, to feel his desire....

"Remy?" she whispered, unable to disguise the longing in her voice. He seemed to freeze, and for what seemed like an eternity of seconds, he didn't answer.

"It's been a long day," he finally said, his voice hoarse and strained. He eased her back onto the bed. "Go to sleep."

She felt him move away, and disappointment, sharp and swift, stung like a slap in the face. Her cheeks grew warm with humiliation. "I just wanted to thank you," she lied.

"I don't think that's exactly what you had in mind, Kendall. But I'm giving you fair warning. I care about you and I want you—I'm only human—but I won't be satisfied with just one night. When I take you to bed, it will be for keeps."

Since there was nothing to say, nothing she could say, Kendall pulled her knees up to her stomach beneath the covers, closed her eyes and prayed for sleep.

WHEN SHE AWOKE the following morning, Remy had already showered and dressed.

He walked to the door. "There's a small doughnut shop down the way, within sight of the motel, and the patrol car is still parked out front. While you dress, I'll pick up some coffee and doughnuts."

Kendall nodded.

"Secure the latch and don't let anyone but me back inside."

Again she nodded, and as soon as he closed the door behind him, she jumped out of bed, hurried over and locked the door.

By the time Remy returned, she'd showered and dressed. There was nothing in Remy's manner or expression to give her a hint of what he was feeling, but his silence was loud and clear. He'd said it all the night before.

Kendall welcomed the strong, hot coffee, but the too-sweet doughnuts left her stomach queasy. Still, she ate two of them just so she wouldn't be obliged to make conversation.

Thirty minutes later, they were in his truck, heading for the swamp-tour headquarters. It had been Remy's suggestion that she leave her car at the motel as a decoy, just in case the guy should come back.

"Before we load the boat, I want to talk to Claudia again," he said as he parked the truck, shoved the gearshift into reverse and switched off the engine. "This should be a good time, since the morning tour has just left."

Kendall trailed along behind Remy into the gift shop. Once inside, he signaled for Claudia to join them in the office.

Kendall sat in a chair off to the side of the desk. When Claudia entered, she nodded at Kendall. "Nice to see you again." Kendall nodded back and smiled.

Remy gestured toward the door as he settled in the chair behind the desk. "Close the door, why don't you? I don't won't any eavesdroppers," he said as he began shuffling through a stack of mail.

Claudia smiled, but the smile didn't quite reach her eyes. "Sure, boss," she replied as she firmly shut the door. "So what's this all about?" She laughed nervously. "You ain't planning on firing me, are you?"

Remy jerked his head up. "No, Claudia," he said evenly. "Why would I do something stupid like that?"

A one-shouldered shrug was the only answer she gave.

"What I need from you is your help. What I'm about to tell you is strictly confidential, just between me and you." He tilted his head toward Kendall. "This lady's life could depend on it." He motioned toward the remaining chair in the small room, and Claudia sat down.

As Remy repeated the story he'd told Jake Trahan, Claudia's expression underwent a metamorphosis of shock, disbelief and finally sympathy. "I need information," he said when he'd finished. "I want you to think back to the day that Ms. Delaney rented the boat. I want to know who was hanging around the gift shop or the dock—anyone who could have seen her leave in the boat.''

Claudia crossed her arms, and for several minutes she didn't speak as she stared thoughtfully up at the ceiling.

"Everything was pretty wild that morning, 'specially when Joey...'' A blush darkened her cheeks. "Anyways, that was the day I had to leave early.'' She paused and her frown deepened. "A couple a tourists showed up just as the boat left and they figured they'd hang around until the next tour. They were from Italy, I think. But all they did was sit on the porch most of the time, and... Oh, yeah, Flora and Desiree was just leaving. Desiree come in to fill up the shelves, and I 'member one of them Italians haggling with Flora over the price of that herb tea Desiree swears is good for arthritis. I think he bought out her whole supply.''

Kendall suddenly froze. Flashes of memory flickered in her head...of a swarthy, gray-haired man gesturing wildly to a striking, middle-aged woman, their voices raised in good-natured bartering. The woman's salt-and-pepper hair was pulled back into a knot at the nape of her neck, but it was the mud-caked rubber boots she was wearing that had drawn Kendall's attention.

And there'd been another woman—an older woman wearing the same kind of boots. Desiree.

No wonder she'd been so confused, so certain she'd met Desiree before, Kendall thought. Desiree hadn't lied when she'd said they had never met, but Kendall remembered seeing the old woman, could even now recall the piercing, unnerving look Desiree had given her, still almost feel the hypnotic effect of the old woman's dark eyes.

Kendall blinked and shivered.

"Hey, are you feeling okay?"

It was Remy's concerned tone that finally got her attention, and she swallowed and nodded.

He frowned. "Are you sure? You look as if you've seen a ghost."

"I—I'm fine," she answered, and tried to smile.

"Oh, yeah!" Claudia interrupted, and since any discussion of Desiree had become such a touchy subject between them, Kendall was relieved when Remy turned his attention back to the young woman.

"I just remembered of someone else I saw that morning. T-boy Melancon come in just when Flora and Desiree was leaving."

Remy tensed and his voice hardened. "Came in from where?"

"I guess from fishing, but now's I think of it, I don't recall seeing no fishing gear." Claudia shrugged. "And once he'd talked to Flora, he left again."

For a second, Kendall saw a glimmer of emotion in Remy's eyes. "He talked to Flora?"

Claudia nodded, then a slow, knowing smile pulled at her lips. "Yeah, and if you ask me, they looked pretty darn chummy. You think they got something going on between them?"

Whatever Remy would have answered was interrupted by the sound of a bell.

"Oops, a customer," Claudia said. "Anyways, that's about all I remember." She stood.

"Go ahead and see to the customer. And Claudia?"

She paused at the door.

"Thanks for the information. I don't know how I'd run this place without you."

Just before the young woman disappeared, Kendall caught a glimpse of her face and a smile as bright as sunshine.

"That was really a nice compliment. It meant a lot to her," she said to Remy.

A dark flush stole across his face and he shifted his gaze to a stack of envelopes in the middle of his desk. If Kendall hadn't known better, she would have sworn that he actually squirmed in his chair. *So the man of steel emotions has a chink in his armor, a soft spot after all,* she thought. For reasons she couldn't begin to fathom, the thought was both comforting and amusing.

"Claudia's a hard worker," he said gruffly before reaching for the telephone and punching out some numbers.

"This is Remy Delacroix," he growled into the receiver. "I need to talk to Jake Trahan."

Kendall sat up straighter in her chair and waited, anxious to hear why he was calling the sheriff.

"Jake? Remy here. I think I finally realized why the perp seemed so familiar. You remember a slime-ball named T-boy Melancon? Well, put him at the top of your suspect list. I've got this gut feeling that he's somehow connected to our problem last night." Remy listened for several seconds before he spoke again. "No, I don't have any hard proof and I'm not sure any of this means a damn. All I know is that he fits the MO and he was sent away for poaching alligators—his second time around. For a while now, I've been chasing a poacher, and up until a few minutes ago, I didn't know T-boy was out on probation or he would have been my number-one suspect.''

The minute Remy hung up the receiver, Kendall pounced on him. "Who is this T-boy Melancon and what has he got to do with last night?''

Remy fixed her with a steady gaze. "I don't have any proof yet, but when Claudia mentioned his name, it suddenly clicked as to why the perp last night seemed familiar. He reminded me of T-boy. And when she mentioned that he'd talked to Flora...well, Flora is into voodoo, too. Her motive for scaring you off is pretty obvious, but I can't see her as a murderer, so now we need to figure out what reason T-boy could have to want you dead.''

Remy cocked his head to one side and narrowed his eyes. "Does any of this ring a bell? Has anything about that day come back to you?''

Kendall lowered her gaze. She could feel Remy's eyes on her, probing, measuring, and for a second she considered sidestepping his question. But only for a second. She never had been good at lying, and she figured that of all people, Remy would see through a lie. And as touchy as the subject was with him, she knew there was no way she could put off discussing Desiree.

She looked him straight in the eyes. "I do recall renting the boat that day, and I also remember seeing the people that Claudia mentioned, although at the time, I had no idea who they were.''

"Including Desiree?"

She nodded. "I saw her but didn't talk to her."

"Do you remember ever seeing any of them before that day?"

She shook her head.

"And you still think Desiree is the one who attacked you?"

Kendall sighed. "I don't know what to think any more. But one thing I do know. I'm tired. Could we please leave now? I think I'd like to take a nap, and I've still got to figure out how I'm going to finish the job I came here to do in the first place." She tapped the cast on her right arm. "Especially with this."

ON THE TRIP BACK to the houseboat, Remy mentally debated what he should do next. Besides the threat to Kendall, he had a promise to keep to Desiree.

His gut instinct was to go after T-boy and beat the truth out of him if he had to, but until he got a lead on him or until he showed up again, Remy knew it would be almost impossible to find him. Other than himself, T-boy was one of the few people who knew the swamp like the back of his hand, and he could hide out indefinitely if he played it smart.

Remy geared down the boat motor, then shut off the engine. As the boat slid in next to the houseboat dock, he decided that the only thing he had any control over was the business with the survey. If Kendall approved the project, and there was a strong probability that she would, he needed to play his ace in the hole. He needed to confront his uncle with Desiree's deed, and hope it would be enough to make him back off.

Kendall went straight to the bedroom once Remy secured the boat, and he started making phone calls as soon as he was sure that she had fallen asleep.

The first call he made was to the Bayou Inn to see which days he could book a reservation for their private dining room. He'd decided that the confrontation with his uncle should be on neutral ground, a public place where Philip was less likely to make a scene.

Remy placed the second call to his uncle Philip.

"Well, my boy. To what do I owe this honor?"

Remy's hand tightened on the receiver. "I need to talk to you. Something has just come to my attention about some family land that I think you ought to know about."

"Well, boy, we're talking, so just spit it out."

"I'd rather tell you in person, so how about lunch one day? My treat. Say at...Bayou Inn?"

"Hmm, I'm pretty busy lately—I don't know..."

"Dad said you wouldn't meet with me," Remy lied, knowing that the one way to get to his uncle was to hint that his brother, Charles, might have a stake in it.

"Charles knows about this?"

Remy smiled. *Bingo!* "Like I said, it's about family land."

"Yes, so you did, my boy. So you did. Let me see, now. Today is Sunday, and according to my calendar, I could probably squeeze lunch in on...say, tomorrow, Monday, around eleven-thirty. That way we can beat the crowd."

"See you tomorrow, then."

Remy depressed the switch, released it and placed a call to Desiree.

"I've set up a meeting with Philip," he told her. "Can you bring the deed and be at Café Beltane at the Bayou Inn for eleven-thirty-five tomorrow?"

"With pleasure," the old woman answered. "Your uncle has much to answer for, and it's past time that he reap what he sowed."

Remy frowned. "What does that mean?"

"Just an old woman's ramblings, *mon garçon.* Nothing to concern yourself with."

Even after he'd hung up the phone, Remy still puzzled over Desiree's strange comments. Not for one moment did he believe what she'd said about the ramblings of an old woman. He'd never known Desiree to say or do anything without purpose.

Remy took a deep breath. Sooner or later, she'd reveal her purpose, but only when she was good and ready. He'd have to wait, but for now, what he needed were witnesses for his meeting with his uncle. Not just one, but several, he decided.

The next call Remy placed was to his father's office. His niece, Shelby, answered. "I need a favor," he said. "I want you, Dad, Brody and Joanna to meet me for lunch tomorrow at the Bayou Inn, eleven-thirty-five sharp. Just tell Dad that I need help with some family business."

## CHAPTER TWELVE

MONDAY MORNING DAWNED clear, bright and cool, though the high for the day was predicted to climb into the seventies.

Outside on the houseboat deck, Remy sipped his first cup of coffee. Early morning was one of his favorite times of day in the swamp. It was almost like being in a cathedral of nature as the sun peeked through the trees, spreading a warm pink glow.

As he watched a pileated woodpecker working away at a dead limb in a sycamore tree and a V formation of mallards wing their way overhead, Remy thought again about Kendall's dilemma. Most of Sunday afternoon had passed quietly, with both of them careful to stay out of the other's way. No small feat, considering their living quarters, he had found.

Then, over an evening meal of soup and sandwiches, she had made her announcement. "I need your help," she'd said. "I'd like to hire you to take me back to Willow Island."

Remy couldn't believe his ears and had almost choked on the bite of sandwich he'd just taken. "You want to *hire* me to help you do a job that could put me out of business?"

"You said yourself that Desiree's deed would

more than likely stop the project, anyway, so what difference does it make?''

He hadn't given her an answer, and at some point during the early hours before dawn, he'd finally concluded that with or without him, she was determined to go back to Willow Island. And the one thing he didn't want and didn't need on his conscience, regardless of the consequences, was the death of another woman.

The rattling of dishes caught his attention, alerting him that Kendall was finally awake. He drained his coffee cup and headed for the kitchen.

Kendall was already dressed, in clothes much the same as the day he'd found her: khaki pants and a cotton blouse.

''Going somewhere?'' he asked as he filled his cup again.

She shot him a murderous look. ''I've decided you're taking me to Willow Island.''

''Oh, you've decided, have you? And just how do you intend to make me?''

''You know I can't make you, but if you don't agree, then I'll call Jake Trahan. I'm sure that once I explain, he'll be willing to send a deputy for me.''

''Tell you what,'' Remy said. ''I'll make you a deal. I'll take you to Willow Island, free of charge, but you have to wait until later this afternoon. I have a lunch appointment, but I should be back by about two. Still plenty of time before sunset.''

The shocked expression on her face was priceless. All the way to the mainland, every time he thought about it, he almost smiled.

WHEN REMY ARRIVED at the restaurant, a hostess he recognized as June Pochet showed him to the small private dining room. The table was set for seven. "This is just great, June. The others should be along shortly."

"If you'll tell me who's coming," she said as she poured him coffee, "I can direct them back here."

Remy nodded. "There will be my father, my uncle Philip, Brody Wagner, my niece Shelby, my cousin Joanna and Desiree Boudreaux."

The startled expression on June's face was almost comical. "Has someone died?"

Remy chuckled and shook his head. "No one has died," he answered, well aware that anyone who had lived in Bayou Beltane for long knew about his father's estranged relationship with his twin brother.

"I'll show them in when they get here, Remy."

Remy sipped his coffee, and within minutes, Philip walked through the door. The moment his eagle eyes took in the place settings he pursed his lips and frowned. "What is this? A party you forgot to tell me about?"

Before he could answer, Remy's other guests, led by Desiree, filed into the room, one behind the other.

Philip glared at Charles, then turned angry eyes on Remy. "What's going on here, boy?" he blustered. "I thought this was a private lunch, just you and me."

Remy gestured toward the chair across from him. "Why don't you sit down, Uncle Philip, and I'll explain."

Again Philip directed a glare at his brother. "I don't think so."

"Don't be asinine, Philip," Charles said evenly. "Believe me, you know as much about this meeting as I do. Just sit down, so we can all learn why my son thought it necessary to have this little family get-together."

Sensing that his uncle was on the verge of walking out, Remy stood. "Uncle Philip—"

Before he had time to make a move, Desiree stepped in front of Philip. "Yes, Philip, do sit down." She reached inside her pocket, pulled out an envelope and slid it back and forth between her fingers. "We have much to discuss today, and you would do well to listen for once in your life."

There wasn't a sound in the room. As if he were hypnotized, Philip stared at the envelope in the old woman's gnarled fingers. Sudden color suffused his face, and he reached up to rub his shoulder.

Sensing that his uncle was determined to leave despite Desiree blocking his way, Remy quickly moved to the old woman's side.

Desiree handed him the envelope, and out of the corner of his eye, Remy spotted June hovering in the doorway, her eyes wide with curiosity. "Would anyone like a drink?" she asked.

"Why don't you give us another few minutes," Remy said. "I'll call you when we're ready to order."

She nodded, then quickly glanced around the room one more time before she disappeared.

Remy cleared his throat. "I asked everyone to meet because it's come to my attention that someone is trying to push through a project aimed at draining the Bayou Beltane swamp so that a big, fancy subdivision can be built.'' He turned his gaze on his uncle. ''I believe that someone to be you, Uncle Philip.''

There were murmurs of disbelief from the others in the room as they formed a loose circle around the two men. Philip straightened his shoulders and lifted his chin a notch. ''And what if it is?'' he challenged.

''Then, you're doing so illegally.'' Remy slipped the deed from the envelope. ''This is a deed to Desiree from my grandfather, giving her forty acres that sit smack in the middle of Delacroix land, the land in question.''

''Impossible,'' Philip whispered, his face flushing to a deeper red. ''That's impossible,'' he repeated louder as he snatched the paper out of Remy's hand, opened it and began reading it.

Remy felt a hand on his shoulder. ''Why didn't you come to me with this before now, son?''

Remy faced his father. ''I only learned about it Saturday,'' he answered evenly.

Suddenly, Philip laughed. ''I can't believe you let this old woman take you in like this. Why, anyone could have written this garbage. It's a fake, of course.'' He glared at Desiree. ''Besides, what earthly reason would my father have to give this much land to her?''

''I don't think it's a fake,'' Remy answered. ''But there are ways of finding out.''

''It's not a fake, Philip.'' Desiree stared up at him. ''And to answer your question, your papa had plenty reason for giving me that land. You were too young to understand or remember, but when you and Charles were just three, your momma, rest her sweet soul, lost a baby—a little male child. I tried to help her keep it, but there was nothing I could do. It was out of my hands, and your momma, she had so much grief that your papa was at his wit's end. So I did the only thing I could.

"You see…I was pregnant, but I was only a young girl of seventeen, and my baby had no papa." The old woman lifted her chin as if defying anyone to pass judgment on her. "I knew my baby was going to be a boy and I wouldn't be able to take care of him, but I loved him and wanted him to have all the things I couldn't give him, so I gave your momma and papa a baby—my baby, and they adopted him. Your brother, William, was my little boy first."

There was a collective gasp, and even Remy found himself too stunned to speak.

"Lies!" Philip yelled. His shook the deed in the old woman's face. "All lies!"

"I'm not the one who tells lies around here," Desiree said softly, her voice eerily strong, her eyes boring into his. "But if you want to talk about liars, then I could say plenty. I know lots of secrets, Philip Delacroix…your secrets."

Philip blanched and sweat popped out on his brow. He reached up and pulled the end of his bow tie to loosen it. "I don't have to stay here and listen to this," he said, and turned toward the door.

"Father?" Joanna hurried to her father and grabbed his arm. Philip tried to shake her loose, but she held on tightly. "You're upset. Let me drive you home!"

"I can drive myself."

"You're not in any condition to drive, so stop being so stubborn."

Philip allowed Joanna to steer him to the door, but there he dug in his heels. "You better watch your step, old woman," he called over his shoulder.

Desiree only smiled serenely. "No, Philip. You had better be watching your own step."

The moment that Philip and Joanna left, pandemonium broke out in the room, with every talking at once.

Outside, Joanna helped her father into the passenger seat of her car. He was still pale and still sweating; it worried her.

"Are you in pain?" she asked as she glanced in the rearview mirror, then pulled out onto the road.

"It's nothing," he answered gruffly.

"Don't be so mule-headed. With the family history of heart problems, you can't afford to ignore symptoms. If you're in pain, maybe I'd better take you to the clinic."

"I'm not in pain, Joanna. I told you it's nothing, so drop it. I'm just upset because of that stunt your cousin pulled."

"If there was no truth in his claim, then why did it upset you so?"

"There is no truth in any of their claims. End of discussion."

"Why not discuss it?" she asked, but the only answer she received was his tight-lipped silence. Minutes later she pulled into her father's driveway, and the second she stopped the car, he pushed open the door and climbed out.

Joanna put the car in gear, switched off the engine and followed her father to the front porch.

At the steps, he suddenly let loose a string of curses, then stopped so abruptly that she almost ran into him.

"Father, what on earth…" She sidestepped around him, and it was then that she spotted the source of his irritation. "Is that what I think it is?" She stared at the strange-looking object lying in the middle of the bottom step.

"Yes, it's a gris-gris," he muttered, bending down and snatching it up.

Joanna frowned. "Why would someone leave such a thing on your front step?"

"I'm sure it's nothing more than some kind of sick joke," he answered, and though he tried to make light of the situation, Joanna suspected that there was more to it than her father was letting on. But from the stubborn expression on his face, she also suspected that, like the accusations that Remy and Desiree had made, this was just one thing more he would refuse to discuss.

ACROSS THE BAYOU, Kendall heard the sound of an approaching boat. She hurried to the kitchen window and peeked out. Even with Remy's assurance that no one would bother her at the houseboat, she was still a bit nervous and jumpy after her near miss back at the motel.

When the boat came into view, she sighed. It was Remy. When she spotted another boat right behind him, her pulse jumped. "Now what do I do?" she muttered, watching as Desiree's boat drew closer.

According to everything they had learned, T-boy Melancon was most probably her attacker, not Desiree—and not Remy, thank God. So how was she supposed to act around the old lady now after her accusations? Other than an apology what could she say to her? All she could do, she decided, was to be polite and civil.

She only hoped that Remy hadn't changed his mind about taking her back to Willow Island. She was still sure the place was the key to the gaps in her memory, and regardless of her feelings for Remy, she still had a job to finish.

The first thing Desiree did when she entered the kitchen was to walk straight to Kendall and give her a brief hug.

"I was wrong," Kendall whispered. "Please forgive me."

Then, with a knowing smile on her lips and an equally knowing look in her dark eyes, the old woman nodded then moved away, stepping over to the stove. "There's nothing to forgive," she said as she filled a kettle with water and set it on the stove to boil. "What you need is a good cup of tea to see things more clearly," she said. "Everything always looks better after a cup of tea."

Kendall was so disconcerted that she hadn't yet moved by the time the old woman had set out three mugs on the counter. "Sit down, Kendall," Desiree said gently. "And you too, Remy. After our tea, you can go about your business."

Once she'd served the tea, Desiree seated herself opposite Kendall. "What is wrong with your mother?"

The question, like the earlier show of affection, caught Kendall off balance once again.

"Depends on which one of her many doctors you talk to." The moment the sarcastic words popped out, guilt, like a sharp knife, sliced at her insides. Kendall bit her bottom lip and lowered her gaze to stare at her cup of tea. When she spoke again, her voice was soft and even. "When her most recent doctor couldn't find anything physically wrong, he diagnosed her problem as being psychosomatic," she said. "He strongly suggested that she should see a psychiatrist."

"And of course your momma assumed he was suggesting she might be crazy?"

Kendall nodded, still remembering the terrible argument they'd had. For years she'd thought that her mother could use some counseling, but just the mention of a shrink had caused her to withdraw for days.

"I would like to take a look at her, talk to her. From what you've said, I think I may be able to help her."

Before Kendall had come to Bayou Beltane and witnessed for herself the healing powers of the old woman, she would have found Desiree's proclamation laughable. But Desiree was respected and revered, and though her cures were unconventional, Kendall had seen the results with her own eyes the day she had made rounds with her. Besides, she thought, what could one more opinion hurt?

"You would do that for me—for my mother, even after I...I—"

"You were confused, child. And scared."

The old woman's gentle dismissal made Kendall

feel both humbled and ashamed. "I don't know what to say."

Desiree smiled. "Can you bring your mother here for a few days?"

Kendall's heart sank. "I'm sure the friend staying with my mother wouldn't mind driving her down, but then what? Even if it was safe for us to stay at the motel, I really can't afford the extra expense."

Desiree lifted her chin. "She can stay with me."

For the first time since the conversation began, Remy intervened. "And where do you plan on her sleeping? There's barely enough room at your house for you and Flora."

The old woman shrugged. "We will work it out. Besides, lately, Flora doesn't come home at night too often, a sure sign that she has a new man."

When Remy suddenly went still and his fingers tightened around his mug, Kendall wondered if he was recalling what Claudia had said about Flora and T-boy.

"Do you know who Flora's new man is?" he asked, staring at Desiree.

The old woman nodded. "I suspect he's the same one you and Jake are searching for."

"Damn," he muttered. "But how—"

"How did I know who you were searching for?" The old woman smiled. "Like I told your uncle, I know lots of things…lots of secrets. I only wish I knew how to deal with that daughter of mine. You know as well as I do how headstrong and heart fool-ish she can be, and I have me a feeling that this man is like the others—no good."

"Do you know where I can find him?"

The old woman shook her head with regret. "*Non,* not yet. But I suspect that Claudia's brother Joey might know."

Remy cursed again, but Desiree turned back to Kendall. "You get your momma here. Like I said, she can stay with me."

"What's wrong with her staying here?"

Remy's sudden query took Kendall completely by surprise, but Desiree's expression turned smug. "I thought you were never going to offer."

Remy sighed and shook his head. "I should have known. That's what you had in mind all along, wasn't it, you old conniver?"

"Among other things." Desiree slid a glance to Kendall and winked. Then she reached over and patted his arm. "You have a good heart, Remy Delacroix." She withdrew her hand, shoved back her chair and stood. "Now that that's settled, finish your tea." She focused on Kendall. "Have your mother's friend bring her soon. But for today, I have patients to tend to, and I think you have some unfinished business on Willow Island, eh?"

As soon as the door closed behind the old woman, Kendall turned to Remy. "Did you tell her we were going to the island?"

Remy's lips stretched into a thin smile. "No."

"Then, how did she know?"

He shrugged. "That's a question I've been asking all of my life. Desiree is—" he shrugged again "—uncannily perceptive, for lack of a better description."

A shivery feeling swept through Kendall, followed swiftly by a strange sort of peace. How could she ever have thought that Desiree would intentionally harm her when the old woman had dedicated her life to healing? Remy had tried to tell her, but she'd been too stubborn to listen…and too scared.

"Remy?" She reached out and covered his hand with hers. "Thank you," she whispered.

As if he'd been hit with a jolt of electricity, he jerked his hand away. "We need to get going," he said gruffly. "And don't thank me too soon." He abruptly stood. "You and your mother are welcome to stay here for as long as it takes, but I'm giving you fair warning. I plan to fight this land thing even if it means taking it to court and the media." His gaze hardened and his eyes turned to slivers of green ice. "And even if it means dragging you, the DES and my uncle through the muck along the way."

# CHAPTER THIRTEEN

TRUE TO HIS WORD, Remy took Kendall to Willow Island. The trip exhausted her, both physically and mentally. When they returned to the houseboat, she placed a call to her mother and arranged for Doris to drive her to Bayou Beltane. They agreed that she'd do so early the next morning.

The next call Kendall placed was to Desiree, who graciously agreed to meet the two women at the gift shop and bring Kendall's mother to Remy's houseboat. The moment Kendall hung up the phone, she quickly excused herself and went straight to bed.

A long time later, Kendall glanced at the glowing numbers of the digital clock sitting on the bedside table. Two hours had passed since she'd bid Remy good-night, two restless hours in which her mind refused to shut down despite the demands of her tired body. Outside, the wild night sounds of the swamp seemed to mock her, and disappointment, sharp and swift, still knifed through her each time she thought about the trip to Willow Island.

She'd had such high hopes, had been so sure that all she needed to do was set foot on the island and the rest of her memory would be magically, instantly restored.

But there had been no instant recollections, and

worse, Remy's every action and every word had been
a poignant reminder of his earlier declaration. He'd
warned her. He'd drawn the lines of loyalties and
made it perfectly clear where his allegiance lay. He'd
said he would fight her if need be, and now she believed him.

Kendall closed her eyes and once again tried the
relaxation techniques that Sam had shown her. He'd
told her to clear her mind by concentrating on a setting or a landscape, something serene, something
beautiful. Then she had imagined being in the midst
of a rolling meadow of wild flowers, but now, as she
finally drifted off to sleep, the mental image subtly
altered to include Remy, his emerald eyes glowing
with love and adoration....

OUTSIDE, REMY PROWLED the length of the houseboat deck like a caged panther, his thoughts in a turmoil. He'd allowed Kendall to badger him into taking her back to the island, and though he didn't doubt
for one moment that she was sincere about finishing
her work, her real purpose for returning to the island
had become evident almost immediately. She had
hoped that seeing the island, actually stepping foot
on it, would be the stimulation she needed to regain
the missing gaps in her memory.

He'd witnessed firsthand her disappointment, and
it had taken every bit of willpower he could muster
to keep his hands off of her and allow her to shut
herself up in the bedroom once they returned, when
all he'd wanted was to hold her, to somehow chase
away the demons of defeat that he'd seen reflected
in her dark eyes.

He'd tried watching television, hoping to block out the sounds of her preparations for bed, but had soon become annoyed and turned it off. Next he'd tried reading, but found himself staring at the words without comprehending their meaning. Finally, like so many other times in his life, he'd resorted to soaking up the atmosphere of the swamp, hoping that it would once again work its magic on his restless soul.

The cries he heard were faint at first, so faint that they blended in with the other night sounds. Thinking that some wild swamp creature had just become another victim of nature's food chain, Remy ignored them. Then they grew louder, and he stopped his pacing to listen. When a cry came again, his pulse jumped and he froze.

*Kendall!*

By the time he reached her bed and switched on the lamp, she was thrashing about, reminding him of the night in the clinic.

He took a firm hold of her shoulders. "Kendall, wake up!" She moaned again and fought him. "Kendall, honey, please."

She suddenly went still, and when she opened her eyes, they were wide with confusion. "Remy? Oh, Remy!" She grabbed him around the neck and clung to him, her body still shaking from the aftermath of the nightmare. "It—it was horrible," she stammered, her voice hoarse with fright. "I was back on the island."

"Hey, sweetheart. It's okay. It was only a nightmare." Remy eased down onto the edge of the bed and held her tightly.

He felt as if someone had wrapped a cold fist

around his heart and was squeezing it. He knew firsthand what it was like to battle night demons, and he
wouldn't wish that horror on anyone, but most especially not on Kendall. At that moment, he would
have given anything to spare her that misery.

All he wanted was to offer comfort, to somehow
help chase away her demons. But as the seconds
ticked by and she finally stopped shivering, it grew
increasingly hard to ignore the warm sensation of her
firm breasts pressed so intimately against his chest.
She was wearing the thin nightgown he'd bought her,
and that realization, along with finally having her in
his arms again, had him rock hard and aching with
need. But for Remy, it wasn't simply a matter of
physical need. With the passing of each day, he'd
begun to realize that he needed her in other ways as
well...all the ways a man needs a woman for a lifetime.

Careful of her cast, he gently but firmly untangled
her other arm from around his neck. "Tell me about
your nightmare," he encouraged gruffly as he set her
away from him. He snagged the extra pillow and
stuffed it behind her.

For seconds she stared at him, a faraway look in
her eyes. "I'm not so sure it was a nightmare. Nightmares tend to fade pretty quickly, but this..." She
bowed her head and clutched the sheet. "I can still
recall every horrible detail."

"Could it have been a memory flash?"

She squeezed her eyes closed. "I—I don't know.
Maybe. It seemed too real to be a nightmare, but
I—I just don't know."

He grasped her chin, gently forcing her to look at

him. "This could be important," he stated, "so tell me about it and don't leave out anything."

The moment he released her, she directed her gaze to a point just beyond his shoulder, and when she finally spoke again, her voice was soft and remote. "I was on Willow Island," she began. "I was checking the location of the stakes against the survey map. I'm not sure just how long I'd been there, but I decided to check things from a different angle. It was when I went farther inland that I heard several popping sounds. At first I ignored it, but then it suddenly dawned on me that what I'd probably heard were gunshots—the kind of sound a .22 calibre makes. All I could think of was that I needed to get away as quickly and as quietly as I could. But when I turned to go back, I spotted…" She shivered and suddenly couldn't seem to find the right words.

"Come on, sweetheart. Tell me what you saw."

She slowly shook her head from side to side. "At first I wasn't sure what I was seeing, so I took a couple of steps closer. Then I—I… What I was seeing were dead animals of some kind. From the shape of them, I guessed they were alligators, but it was hard to tell since they were so—so mangled and bloody."

Remy groaned. "I should have known…should have realized from the beginning—poachers. You probably stumbled on some poachers. Just shooting the gators doesn't kill them—it only stuns them. Once the hunters get them out of the water, they chop the back of the alligator's neck with an ax and the gator bleeds to death."

"No," she whispered, her eyes again growing

wide with horror. "I mean yes, but I think there was only one—one poacher. I remember hearing a noise behind me, and when I turned, this man was standing there. The last thing I remember was the butt of his gun coming at me."

The mental picture she'd drawn was brutally graphic, and raw fury welled up in Remy, making his voice harsh. "Can you describe the man who hit you?"

Kendall flinched, then bowed her head and squeezed her eyes closed. "Just his face," she whispered. "I'll never forget that face. It was hard, weathered-looking, all sharp angles with a scar across his cheek. And his eyes..." She shuddered. "Blacker than black. He was wearing one of those army camouflage caps, and beneath it, his hair...I remember that his hair was gray, long and kind of stringy, like it needed washing."

Remy bit back another curse. "T-boy," he growled.

Kendall nodded. "Now that you mention it, the man in my nightmare did look a lot like the man I saw talking to Desiree and Flora the day I rented the boat."

"This has to be a memory, not just a nightmare. T-boy is up to his old tricks again. No wonder he left you for dead. He's a two-time loser. Another conviction would send him to prison for life this time. But what I can't figure out is how he knows you survived or how he knew you were at the motel...unless—" He closed his eyes and groaned. "Flora!" He spat out the name. "Claudia said they were acting chummy, and if what Desiree suspects about Flora's absences is true, then she's the only one I can think of who had reason to tell him. Hell, she might even be in cahoots with T-boy's poaching activities.''

"But that still doesn't explain the voodoo doll in the motel that first day. It was left before I ever saw what he was doing. And no one but my boss knew I was coming here.''

"Did you make a reservation?''

Kendall nodded slowly.

"And did you use your own name or the department's?''

Remy saw her visibly swallow. "The DES,'' she whispered, then she shook her head. "It still doesn't makes sense, though. The timing is all wrong. What reason would Flora have to leave the voodoo doll before I stumbled on this T-boy's poaching activities?''

Remy frowned thoughtfully. What reason indeed? he wondered. "The only thing I can think of is that Flora knew what a favorable assessment could mean.'' He shook his head. "But somehow I can't picture her being that civic-minded. There has to be more to it.'' He paused, then shook his head again. "I don't have all the answers yet,'' he finally said. "But now that I know for sure who tried to murder you, I will have them, just as soon as I catch the son of a bitch.''

The murderous look on Remy's face was frightening, leaving no doubt as to his intentions, and even though Kendall was well aware that he'd been a cop, all she could think about was that he could get hurt.

"We need to call Jake Trahan," she said, praying that Remy would agree.

"You're right, we do need to call him."

For a moment, Kendall's hopes soared, but when she ventured a glimpse into Remy's eyes, her hopes plummeted.

"I'll call him," Remy said in a dangerous tone of voice, "but only after I find T-boy and get my answers."

Kendall didn't think, she simply reacted. She reached out and traced the hard line of his beard-roughened jaw with her fingers. "Please don't go after him by yourself," she pleaded. "I couldn't stand it if anything happened to you." And she meant it with all her heart. What she didn't tell him, couldn't tell him yet, was that as unlikely as it seemed, she'd suddenly realized that she had done what would probably turn out to be a very foolish thing—somewhere along the way, she had fallen in love with him.

For what seemed an eternity, Remy didn't move as he stared at her. Kendall didn't try to hide her newfound love, but stared back at him boldly. Then, almost reluctantly it seemed, as if he couldn't help himself, he reached up and traced the line of her lips, and for a split second she could almost believe that she saw her own love reflected in the depths of his eyes.

Then he pulled away, and though it hurt, she tried to ignore the pain of his rejection. But had the brief flare of emotion in his eyes been rejection or love and desire?

Kendall had never been good at second-guessing.

She ruthlessly pushed aside her pride and braced herself. "I care about you, Remy. I—I love you," she whispered brokenly.

At first he didn't answer, and as the seconds dragged by, her heartbeat slowed to a thudding ache. Then suddenly, with a groan of pure animal need, he grabbed her and pulled her roughly into his arms. When his mouth covered hers, she felt an explosion of passion such as she'd never experienced before. There was nothing gentle or sweet in the way he ravaged her mouth. It was a raw kiss of possession, of domination, and Kendall surrendered willingly, returning the kiss with a fierceness she hadn't known she was capable of.

She clawed at the back of his shirt, wanting only to get her hand beneath it, to feel his flesh. He suddenly pulled away, and he was breathing hard as he stared deeply into her eyes. "I want you, but I don't want to hurt you. Are you sure?"

At first she was confused. Then he lightly tapped her cast with his knuckles and she understood.

"Please don't stop now. I don't think I could bear it if you stopped."

He cupped her face with his hands. "Oh, lady, do you have any idea what you do to me?" he murmured against her lips.

When Kendall reached down and boldly traced the zipper of his bulging jeans from bottom to top with her fingers, he inhaled sharply, then jerked away and stood.

Sudden doubts assailed her. "Where are you going?"

"Not far," he said hoarsely, backing toward the

adjoining bathroom. She heard a drawer open and shut and then he was back. He dropped a small foil package onto the table and comprehension dawned on her. Once again, as he'd done since the first time she'd laid eyes on him, he was protecting her.

Love for him filled her and spilled over like a warm waterfall. That he could put her well-being before his own driving need was a rare gift, but then one of the many things she'd learned in the past week was that Remy Delacroix was a rare man.

It took him only seconds to strip off his shirt and pull off his jeans and underwear, and when he was finally standing before her, completely naked, Kendall stared at him with shameless fascination. He was whipcord lean, and as her eyes traveled down his broad, hair-covered chest to the evidence of his desire, the sight stirred something deep within her womb. He was hard and ready for her, and knowing that she was responsible was more powerful than any seduction he could have offered.

Ordinarily Kendall preferred sleeping in an oversize T-shirt, but for tonight, for this moment, she was glad that she had worn the gown Remy had given her. Her blood throbbed in her veins, and something pagan within her surfaced. In a ritual that had been passed down through women since time began, she began her own act of seduction.

She kicked away the sheet and got to her knees. With her gaze locked with his, she reached up and slowly, deliberately, loosened each of the tiny pearl buttons that held the gown together over her breasts. Her nipples were already pebbly hard, and her breasts felt full. With a provocative shrug, she let the gown slip off her shoulders, to pool around her hips, and when his gaze shifted to her breasts, she automatically arched her back in a silent offering.

As if in slow motion, he kneeled before her, and very gently, with a butterfly touch, he stroked one finger back and forth over first one nipple, then the other. The ache between her legs grew, and she shivered with need. But the anticipation of his mouth on her breasts was nothing compared to the exquisite reality. He cupped each breast with his hands, and as his lips and tongue laved each nipple, alternately sucking and licking, passion exploded deep inside her. She clutched at his shoulder to brace herself. She couldn't think or reason, could only feel as spasms of desire shot through her.

When he finally lifted his head, his eyes glittered with his own sexual arousal. In one smooth motion, he came up off the floor and pressed his body against hers, until she was lying beneath him between his elbows, staring up at him. Gentleness was the last thing she wanted at the moment, and she silently cursed the cast on her broken arm, which made him so cautious.

But caution came at a price. His skin was hot and slick against her own, and she could feel his sex, hard and even hotter against her thigh. With a groan of sheer need, his mouth covered hers, and her fingers tangled in his hair and tightened. The kiss left her breathless and enveloped her in an all-consuming desire to be filled with him, to be so close that nothing separated them. His tongue darted in and out, mimicking the very act she craved.

"Oh, Remy," she cried. "Now...please, now."

She writhed beneath him, but he shifted away for a moment.

"Hold on, baby." Within seconds he had sheathed himself and was back, hovering over her. "Now tell me again. Tell me what you want."

"I want you," she whispered, arching toward him. "I want you in me, a part of me."

Sweat popped out on his brow and his eyes were like sparkling emeralds, glittering with the fires of passion. He reached down and parted her thighs with his hand, and with one smooth thrust, he entered her.

He filled her totally and completely. She wanted it to last, wanted to feel this way forever, but it was too much. Her body was too ripe and responsive to his every touch. He had no sooner set up a rhythm when suddenly stars burst behind her eyelids, and with a cry of ecstasy, she spiraled out of control.

A harsh cry tore from his throat, he plunged one last time and together they hurled off the edge of the universe, in a climax that left them both trembling in its wake.

WHEN HE WAS FINALLY ABLE to move, Remy eased off of Kendall and lay down beside her. He felt her watching him, and though he knew what she needed from him, he couldn't say the words she wanted to hear—not yet, maybe not ever.

*Bastard.*

The accusation whispered through his mind and guilt stirred his conscience. He shouldn't have given in, shouldn't have made love to her with so many unresolved issues between them. For one thing, they still knew very little about each other, but from what he could determine, they were from two different worlds. For another thing, she was still determined to do the job she'd been sent to do, and there was no way in hell he would allow the swamp he'd loved all of his life to be turned into a damn high-priced housing development.

As if sensing what he was thinking, Kendall turned away, but not before he caught a glimpse of hurt and disappointment in the depths of her eyes.

*Beautiful, beautiful brown eyes...*

Something dark and painful twisted in his gut, and because he couldn't help himself, he reached out and gathered her close, pulling her snugly against his chest. At first she lay stiff and unyielding within his arms, but slowly, he felt the tension ease.

"Remy?"

"Go to sleep, sweetheart," he whispered. "We'll talk in the morning. I promise."

It was a long time before she finally fell asleep, her breathing deep and even, and even longer before Remy was able to doze off. And in those quiet moments, he savored the feel of her naked body pressed close to his, knowing it could well be the first and last time he would be privileged to do so. She was like an aphrodisiac. Even now, his desire stirred and he wanted her again, and he feared it was the kind of wanting that would never leave him for as long as he lived.

Ruthlessly, he pushed away the thoughts of how good she'd been, how right she felt in his arms. He'd slipped up once and given in, but it was a mistake he couldn't afford to repeat....

Remy awoke just before dawn, and calling himself

a coward, he quietly eased out of bed. He'd promised her they would talk, and though he hadn't exactly lied to her, he hadn't told the whole truth, either. They would talk, but not before he did what he had to do. After one last, lingering look at Kendall, he slipped silently out of the room.

In the other bedroom, he quickly dressed and went about gathering what he needed. Though she had asked him to call Jake Trahan, Remy had no doubt that, with or without his consent or cooperation, she intended to do so herself. Whether he did or didn't call the sheriff was no longer an issue of trust. But Jake would be bound by an oath and his badge to do everything by the book, whereas Remy had no such compunctions.

Right now, what he needed was information and time—information on the whereabouts of T-boy and time to track him down. With any luck, Kendall would sleep late, just late enough to give him the head start he needed before she called the police.

Remy stared at the phone sitting on his desk in the living room. Just in case Kendall didn't sleep late, he needed some way to delay her calling Jake. Unplugging the phone and hiding it seemed to be the logical answer, but he quickly decided doing so wasn't a good idea. If something happened to him, he didn't want her stranded. He'd just have to take a chance that he would have enough time to do what he had to.

Hefting his gear over his shoulder, he headed for his boat. For now, he had more to worry about than phone calls.

By the time Remy was in sight of Desiree's house,

the pink hues of dawn were beginning to spread across the horizon. Like him, Desiree lived in the swamp, and the only way in or out was by boat.

Built on piers, the four-room, wood-frame house was old and in dire need of repair. Typical of shotgun shacks, there were no hallways, but each room opened into the next with the doorways perfectly aligned, so that if a man stood at the front door and fired a shotgun, the pellets could travel straight through and out the back door without ever hitting a wall.

Remy cut the motor and paddled around to the rickety pier. When he recognized Flora's boat alongside Desiree's, he figured that his luck was holding, since she was his sole purpose for coming in the first place. He had just tied up his boat when the front door swung open and Flora emerged. She was decked out in her usual cotton shirt, jeans and swamp boots, and she was carrying a canvas bag. Remy figured he'd caught her just as she was leaving on one of her herb- and root-gathering forages.

She spotted him immediately, and though nothing in her expression gave him a clue as to what she was thinking, her animosity toward him was a palpable energy that seemed to reach out and touch him. Evil, he thought. Pure evil, if such a thing existed.

Remy had often wondered how Flora had turned out to be so bad with Desiree as a mother. The only conclusion he'd come to was that she must have gotten an overload of bad genes from some other ancestor along the way. Either that or it was as simple and complex as the difference between good and evil, since even Satan himself was at one time one of God's highest angels.

He had never much cared for Flora, and he knew the feeling was mutual. Because of Desiree, they were polite to each other, but even Flora's politeness had an edge. At sixty-two, she was still a striking woman, but Remy had found that looks were deceiving where she was concerned. There was a sinister and forbidding quality about the embittered, selfish woman. Rumors of her dealings in black magic were widespread, and she seemed to take an ungodly pleasure in her ability to frighten people.

As he approached her, Remy nodded a stilted greeting.

"My mother is still sleeping," she said, her voice cool and detached. "You'll have to come back later."

"I didn't come to see your mother. I came to see you."

Flora narrowed her eyes. "We have nothing to say to each other."

"Maybe, maybe not. But I have some questions for you."

Her guarded look turned wary. "What kind of questions?" she asked. "But more to the point, what makes you think I would answer anything you might ask?"

Remy straightened to his full, imposing height and glared down at her. "You will," he assured her dangerously. "Either to me or to Jake Trahan, but one way or the other, you will answer."

For the first time he could remember, he thought

he saw a glitter of fear flicker in her dark eyes, but it was too brief for him to be certain.

"Well, ask away," she invited snidely. "But do it quickly. Unlike a lot of you rich people, I have to work for a living."

Remy's hackles rose, but he ignored her sarcastic barb. "Where can I find T-boy Melancon?"

For a moment Flora seemed taken aback, then she raised her chin. "How should I know?"

"Oh, you know all right, so you might as well tell me now."

For an answer, Flora raised an eyebrow and simply stared at him.

A menacing smile pulled his lips into a grim line. "Accessory to attempted murder is a serious charge, Flora," he taunted. "For your mother's sake, I'd hate to think of you spending your retirement days in prison."

"You're bluffing, rich man!" she snarled. "You have no authority here or anywhere else, not since those good old boys in New Orleans made a fool out of you and killed your woman. You didn't have any proof against them, and you don't have a shred of proof that I've done anything wrong or else I would be talking to Jake instead of you."

Remy took a step toward her and his smile turned sinister. "Oh, I had the proof back then," he said, his tone deadly. "What I didn't have was the smarts to realize just how rotten that barrel of apples was. But you're a different barrel, and I've wised up. Proof or no proof, if anything happens to Kendall Delaney, I can promise that I'll *personally* come after you." He took another step that brought him to within a foot of her. "I'm warning you. Keep your goddamned voodoo dolls to yourself from now on, and I'd advise you to tread lightly, because I *will* be watching you."

With one last, menacing glare, he did an about-face and stalked away. At the end of the pier near his boat, he paused. "And one more thing, Flora," he called over his shoulder. "I will find T-boy. Sooner or later, with or without your help, I'll find him," he repeated for emphasis. "And when it comes down to it, which one of you do you think he'll throw to the wolves?" Remy didn't wait for an answer, but got in his boat and left.

He really hadn't expected Flora to tell him where he could find T-boy, but his little visit had accomplished one of its purposes. For all of her failings, Flora wasn't a stupid woman. Remy was pretty sure that she would heed his warning and back off. There would be no more voodoo-doll threats. As for his other purpose for the visit, he was also fairly certain that she would head straight to T-boy to warn him. It would be tricky, since sound carried over the water, but all Remy had to do was watch and wait for her to lead him to the bastard.

Once he was out of sight around a bend, Remy slowly revved down his outboard motor, bit by bit, and hoped that the fading noise would fool Flora into thinking that he was still traveling away from Desiree's house, down the bayou.

There were only two directions that Flora could go. Just in case she came his way, he chose a thick stand of bald cypress to hide in, carefully maneuvering the boat into the center of the grove. He'd just cut the power when he heard the roar of Flora's out-board spring to life. He cocked his head and listened intently, trying to get a feel for which direction she was taking.

From the fading sound of her engine, he quickly determined that she was headed up the bayou in the opposite direction. Luckily for him, that part of the swamp had only a few channels feeding into it, and it had multiple twists and turns, so it would be much easier to follow without being detected.

With his ears fine-tuned to the sound of her motor, Remy began the intricate task of tracking her, trying to harmonize the sound of his outboard with hers. If she slowed, he slowed. If she sped up, he did, too.

He estimated that fifteen minutes of the cat-and-mouse chase had passed before she changed direction. In his mind's eye, he saw her turning at Muskrat Point, down one of the channels leading off the main bayou. Just as he approached the point, he heard her cut her outboard engine, and cursing softly, he immediately did the same.

There were several fishing camps located down the narrow channel, but choosing the one she'd gone to was a problem. Remy picked up a paddle, dipped it deep in the murky water and pulled, quietly guiding his boat toward the first camp.

He was within sight of the camp when, even though there was no sign of Flora's boat, a nagging feeling began gnawing at his insides. Like the blind-ing flash of a light bulb being switched on, a fact suddenly hit him. The third camp down the channel belonged to Claudia's father and brothers, one of three they owned. Desiree had said that T-boy was a

friend of Claudia's brother Joey. She'd also said that
Joey might know where T-boy was hiding out.
"Birds of a feather," he muttered grimly, digging
deeper into the water with his paddle.

The Landrys' fishing camp was even more shoddy
and rundown than Desiree's house, and as he'd suspected, Flora's boat, along with another one, was
moored at the pier.

Remy maneuvered his craft closer to the shoreline,
where he hoped the tall marsh grass would provide
sufficient cover to conceal his presence. He tied it to
a nearby bush and settled back to wait, with nothing
but hungry mosquitos and his thoughts of Kendall to
keep him company. Was she still asleep…in his bed?
Or had she awakened by now and realized he was
gone?

*Please don't go after him by yourself…I couldn't
stand it if anything happened to you…I love
you…love you….* Her words haunted him, like dark
echoes from the depths of his soul. He hadn't asked
for her love, had tried to keep his distance, but in
spite of everything, she'd freely given it.

Would she still feel the same way when she awoke
and found him gone?

## CHAPTER FOURTEEN

IT WAS THE SOUND of an outboard motor that finally awakened Kendall. Bright sunlight was peeping through the blinds, but beside her, the bed was empty and the sheets where Remy had slept were cold. At first she thought that the sound was Remy's boat, that he was leaving without telling her. When the noise of the motor abruptly died, Kendall suddenly realized that someone was arriving, not leaving.

With a frown, she threw back the sheet. It suddenly hit her that the person outside could be T-boy Melancon, and Kendall almost panicked.

*Clothes,* she thought frantically, glancing around the room. She had to get some clothes on. Dressing was awkward with her right arm in a cast, and it usually took her several minutes. She was yanking on a pair of shorts when it finally dawned on her that instead of T-boy, Remy could have left earlier and was now returning.

The sound of sudden laughter reached her ears. Kendall instantly recognized the voices of her mother and Desiree, and feeling a bit foolish for having forgotten about her mother's arrival, she groaned.

She glanced at the clock. "Yep," she muttered. "Eleven o'clock on the dot. Right on time as scheduled."

So where was Remy? she wondered as she headed for the kitchen, trying to zip up her shorts. Kendall didn't have long to wonder. The sight of her mother coming through the door pushed everything else from her mind.

Kendall had grown up with everyone telling her she was the spitting image of her mom. Though there was still a strong resemblance, her mother's battle with weight loss due to her illnesses had taken its toll.

"You've lost more weight," Kendall exclaimed, noting that she looked even more emaciated than usual.

After hugging her daughter briefly, Della Delaney pulled away and dismissed her concern with a wave of her hand. "Maybe a couple of pounds, but I've been so worried about you that I just haven't been hungry. Here…" Before Kendall had time to protest, she reached for the stubborn zipper on her daughter's shorts. "Let me do that." Then she patted Kendall's cheek. "There. Now, where is this nice young man that Desiree has been telling me about? I believe she said that his name is Remy."

"I don't know…exactly," Kendall hedged.

For the first time since she'd entered the room, Desiree spoke. "Did he not come back?"

Kendall tilted her head. "Come back? From where?"

"He was by my house at the break of dawn, talking to Flora. But before I could catch him, he'd already left."

A whisper of terror ran through Kendall.

"Oh, dear! Kendall, what's wrong?"

"It's nothing, Mom," she forced herself to say as she shook her head and tried to control the fear that was spreading like wildfire in her veins. He'd promised they would talk, but instead he'd gone after T-boy. She was sure of it.

Kendall took one look at her mother and knew she needed more reassurance. Kendall didn't think she had the strength to deal with one of her mother's weak spells at the moment. "Nothing for you to worry about," she said in the most reassuring tone she could muster. "It's just that I—I haven't had breakfast yet." For lack of a better explanation, it was the best excuse she could come up with on the spur of the moment.

Kendall quickly turned away and, with trembling fingers, opened the refrigerator. "Why don't I fix us a bite to eat while you freshen up a bit, and you can tell me all about your trip."

"Which way is the bathroom, hon?"

Kendall gestured toward the door to the living room. "Through there and down the hall." She watched until her mother disappeared, then bent down and took out a carton of eggs and a package of bacon. When she straightened and closed the door, she sensed Desiree's presence directly behind her. The old woman placed her hand on Kendall's shoulder.

"Remy will be okay," she said. "He's tough and he's smart. A lot smarter than that *bon à rien*, T-boy Melancon. And another thing." Desiree squeezed Kendall's shoulder. "If he took you to bed—which I suspect he did—then he cares. Why else do you think he went after T-boy?"

Kendall whirled to face the old woman. "How do you do that?"

Desiree raised an eyebrow. "If you mean how do I know he took you to bed, then the answer is that I can still smell him on you. Each person has a distinct scent and you're covered with his."

Kendall felt as if her cheeks were suddenly on fire, and a denial was on the tip of her tongue. But the old woman was right. From the beginning Kendall had loved the way Remy smelled, and his distinct odor of male and musk did still cling to her.

"Oh, sweetheart, you *must* be ill," Della said as she entered the room once again, saving Kendall from having to comment on Desiree's observation. "One minute you're white as a sheet and now you're all flushed." She bustled over and felt Kendall's forehead. "You're not feverish. Maybe you're coming down with the flu?"

If possible, Kendall felt her face grow even hotter with embarrassment. "I'm fine, Mother," she said as she backed toward the cabinet with the eggs and bacon. "Just fine," she mumbled. As if sensing Kendall's dilemma, Desiree stepped in and began questioning Della about her health.

As she prepared breakfast, Kendall was aware of the conversation going on between the two women, but her thoughts were in a turmoil. Regardless of what Desiree had intimated, Kendall was almost certain that Remy would have gone after T-boy, anyway. He might care about her, might even love her, but he didn't trust her, not enough to discuss his plans beforehand.

Kendall removed the sizzling bacon from the frying pan. She figured she had two choices: she could either wait for Remy and do nothing, or she could call Jake Trahan and apprise him of the situation. She turned the burner down and drained the bacon grease into an empty can. If only her choice about writing a favorable assessment was as cut-and-dried, she thought. Either way, she still had a job to do, a position she couldn't afford to lose.

She glanced down at her plaster-encased arm, and after only a moment's hesitation, decided that though she might be able to handle a boat with just one good arm, it would be foolish to do so. Too much could happen in the swamp, and it was too risky with T-boy still running loose. What she needed was someone reliable with a boat and motor. After all, there was safety in numbers, wasn't there? And the sooner she finished her job in Bayou Beltane, the sooner she could get on with the rest of her life.

Though it was a bit awkward, Kendall managed to crack five eggs into a bowl. In the middle of beating them together, she paused, fork in midair. An empty ache began in the pit of her stomach and spread. How could it be that after only a week, it was impossible to imagine never seeing Remy again, never hearing his voice? Never feeling his arms around her, his lips on hers...

Sudden tears sprang into her eyes and she blinked rapidly in an attempt to hold them at bay. For years she'd put her own life, her own needs and wants on hold, so that she could care for her mother. She'd done so partially out of guilt and partially because she hadn't felt that she had the time a relationship would require. She'd never truly thought about the toll it had taken on her and she'd never allowed herself to dwell on what she might possibly be missing in life. Until now. Falling in love with Remy had been the catalyst that brought it to a head.

How ironic, she thought. She'd finally found someone who could make her rise above her guilt and come out of her cocoon, only to realize that a relationship between them was hopeless. Even if they weren't at odds over her approval of the survey, his attitude after they had made love was enough to convince her that he was incapable of trust and commitment. It still hurt each time she thought of her own naiveté, and of how she'd waited to hear words of love afterward only to be heartbreakingly disappointed.

Kendall poured the eggs into the sizzling pan, and as she watched the mixture bubble and cook, she made herself a silent vow. If there was to be any sort of relationship between them at all, Remy Delacroix would have to make the next move.

Once they had finished breakfast, Kendall broached the subject of needing help with Desiree. "I need someone reliable with a boat and a motor to assist me while I finish my work," she told the old woman.

"Oh, honey," her mother exclaimed. "Do you think that's such a good idea?" She reached out and gently touched Kendall's cast. "Are you sure you're up to doing that yet?"

Kendall smiled sadly. "I don't have a choice, Mother," she said. "But please don't worry. I'll be fine." After a moment, she turned back to Desiree. "Can you help me?"

Desiree pursed her lips and tilted her head to one side. "For how long?"

"Just a couple of days. Three at the most."

"Hmm..." The old woman nodded thoughtfully. "I will take you." She turned her head and, with a cunning look in her faded eyes, stared at Della. "Me and your mother. It will be good for her."

Della Delaney gasped. "I couldn't possibly do such a thing. I—I have to—"

"Do you want to get better?" The expression on Desiree's face hardened, as if she were daring Della to say no.

Della looked affronted. "Why, of course I do. Why else would I have come?"

"Why indeed?" Desiree murmured, and ignoring the spark of anger in Della's eyes, she gave a nod of satisfaction. "Then, part of my treatment includes lots of fresh air and sunshine. You need to get out into the world more instead of staying cooped up in a stuffy house with nothing to think of but your aches and pains."

Kendall wanted to stand up and cheer, but she held her breath, instead. For years she'd thought the same thing, and for years the doctors had been giving her mother the same advice. But the few times she'd actually tried to plan an outing, her mother always had one of her spells, and Kendall would end up being swamped with guilt.

"I—I don't feel so good," Della whispered, splaying her hand over her heart. "The drive down and the boat ride might have been too much. I think I need to lie down and rest for a while."

Kendall wanted to groan out loud. If her mother

followed her usual pattern, by morning she would claim to be too ill to get out of bed.

"What you need is to start taking my tonic," Desiree said, reaching into her pocket and pulling out a small paper packet. "Kendall, brew your mother a cup of tea and stir this in, along with a little sugar and milk." She handed Kendall the packet, then turned her attention back to Della. "Drink all of the tea she gives you, then lie down for an hour or so. I'm going to leave another dose for you to take before you go to bed tonight." She pulled another packet out of her pocket and laid it on the table.

An apprehensive frown formed on Della's face as she stared at the packet. "I don't take milk in my tea, and what's in that?" She pointed to it.

"The milk is necessary," the old woman said matter-of-factly. "And as for the ingredients, it's a special mixture of roots and herbs to build up your blood and stamina. It's perfectly safe. I've used it hundreds of times and most of my patients have had good recoveries." Desiree abruptly stood. "I have to leave now, but I'll be back first thing tomorrow morning." She walked toward the door, then paused. "One more thing, Della. I cannot help you if you're not willing to help yourself, and that includes following all of my instructions. I expect you to be dressed and ready to go with us in the morning."

Later that evening, as Kendall stood staring at the bed she'd shared with Remy, she found herself recalling the night before in vivid detail. The sheets were still rumpled and tangled, and there was still an indention in the pillow next to hers.

She reached down and gathered up the pillow and

breathed deeply. His scent still clung to it, bringing to mind what Desiree had said earlier. But now, instead of being embarrassed, Kendall felt tears prick her eyes. Where was he? she wondered. Why hadn't he returned yet? At this very moment, was he in the swamp somewhere, hurt? Or worse, dead—another of T-boy's victims?

Kendall climbed into the bed, and after pulling the covers up to her chin, curled into a fetal position, clutching Remy's pillow to her breasts. She never had called Jake Trahan. Something within her, some sixth sense, had warned her that Remy didn't want police help or he would have called himself. But even if she'd decided to call, it seemed as if she hadn't had a chance to do so all day.

Most of the time her mother was manageable and seemed genuinely cooperative. Only now that Kendall's eyes had been opened did she realize the toll that caring for her mother had taken on her over the years. Always before, she had made excuses for her mother, had been cowed by her own guilt about the part she had played in her mother's financial situation. But it seemed that lately, her mother was getting worse. More and more she required constant supervision.

Despair welled up inside Kendall, and she squeezed the pillow tighter. In spite of everything, she loved her mother, and Desiree was her last resort. If the old woman couldn't help, then Kendall was afraid she might have to do something drastic. For the first time since her father's death, she finally let herself consider the possibility of placing her mom in some kind of home for the elderly, something she had once vowed she would never do.

ACROSS THE BAYOU, Desiree sat in her rocking chair, waiting. She'd left one small lamp burning, and since she didn't hold with all the modern noise of television and radio, except for the night sounds of her beloved swamp and the ticking of the small clock on the end table beside her, all was quiet in her home.

The sound of a boat approaching from far across the peaceful swamp signaled that her waiting was finally over.

The moment that Flora entered the room, Desiree made her presence known. "I want to talk to you," she said, and even in the dim light, she could detect the startled surprise in her daughter's dark eyes. "You thought if you waited long enough, I would be asleep, didn't you?"

Flora went perfectly still, and ignoring her mother's last question, addressed the first one. "Why would you want to talk with me? We've had little to say to each other for years now."

"Don't play your games with me and don't try to change the subject. Your personal vendetta against Philip Delacroix is one thing. With or without your help, one way or another, he will reap what he has sowed. But you are to stay away from Kendall Delaney."

Flora's face flushed in anger. "Why? Because your love-potion tea finally worked and your precious Remy has the hots for her? Well, too bad. I can't take the chance that she will approve Philip's project. All I meant to do was scare her off, so stick to your love potions and mind your own business, old woman."

Desiree's expression didn't alter by even a twitch of a muscle, but she slowly rose to her feet, and her piercing eyes bore into those of her daughter's. "And you need to remember your place, *ma petite*, as well as who and what I am." The threat was spoken softly, but the underlying message was forged with steel and hung in the air between the two women like dark, threatening clouds. "I have looked into the future and have seen T-boy Melancon's fate. He's going down, and unless you want him dragging you with him, keep away from him."

Flora narrowed her eyes and, in a silent challenge, held her mother's gaze in a contest of wills. Outside the small shack, thunder rumbled in the distance and the wild cacaphony of swamp creatures abruptly ceased.

Inside the shack, Flora began shivering uncontrollably, and with a soft cry, finally acknowledged her mother's greater power by being the first to break the deadlock and look away.

TWO DAYS HAD PASSED without a word from Remy. "Where is he?" Kendall cried, unable to hide the desperation that had been building within her, like a volcano on the verge of eruption.

Desiree took her time answering. "He will show up when he's finished with his business," she finally replied calmly, pouring some tea she had brewed and stirring yet another packet of her mysterious tonic into the cup. She tapped the spoon against the edge of the mug, placed the spoon on the counter, then handed the steaming brew to Kendall.

"But what if he—"

"I would know if something happened to him. Now, stop your fretting and take this to your mother, then finish that report you've been working on. I can't wait around all day, so if you want to catch a ride with me to the mainland, either finish it or you're going to be stranded here. I'm leaving within the hour."

It was on the tip of her tongue to question how Desiree would know about Remy, but Kendall figured it was an exercise in futility to even ask. Besides, the old woman was right. She did have a report to finish, and she had been procrastinating all morning.

It had taken Kendall only two days to check out the placement of the stakes and conduct a formal assessment, and her report and stamp of approval should have been simple. What she hadn't counted on was coming face-to-face with the environmental devastation of the wetlands that was sure to follow once the swamp was drained, something that Desiree was quick to point out at every turn.

True to her word, for the past two mornings Desiree had shown up and taken Kendall, along with her mother, around to where the different stakes were located. But they'd spent the afternoons watching Desiree gather and process the different natural ingredients that she used in her teas and medicinal potions, while Kendall spent the evenings writing her report.

She knew that if she wanted to keep her job, she

had no choice but to approve the project. She also kept recalling what Remy had told her about all the people who would be affected if the swamp were lost. But hearing and seeing were two different things. She'd heard what Remy had said, but the more she saw with her own eyes, the more doubts plagued her.

She paused in the doorway of the extra bedroom, and for a moment, she simply stood and watched as her mother went about packing her suitcase. Desiree had suggested that while Kendall was gone to file her report, it might be a good idea for Della to stay with her instead of staying alone on Remy's house-boat. That way, Desiree could make sure that Della followed all of her treatment instructions.

There had been no miracle cure, and her mother still complained of various aches and pains, the same ones that had baffled each of her many doctors for years. But there had been a change, a subtle altering in her mother's mental state and general attitude. It was almost as if she took the aches and pains in stride now and was determined to keep going in spite of them. Thanks to Desiree and her bullying, along with the fresh air, sunshine and daily doses of herbs, thought Kendall.

"Mom, here's your tea."

Della turned and, with a smile, took the cup. "You know," she said, a conspiratorial tone in her voice, "I think I'm beginning to like milk in it, after all, but don't tell Desiree."

A smile tugged at Kendall's lips. Her mother's attempt at humor was yet another welcome change she'd begun to notice. "I won't tell," she assured her. "Are you about ready?"

Della nodded. "But are you?"

Kendall frowned, not exactly sure what her mother was asking.

"Have you made up your mind yet...about that swamp project?"

"What about it?" Kendall said, temporizing.

"Well, I hope you're not thinking about approving it."

"Mom, you don't understand—"

"I understand more than you think I do, and if you're worrying about losing your job, then don't." She set the cup of tea on a nearby table and reached out to clasp her daughter's hand. "Following your heart and doing the right thing is more important."

Kendall firmly removed her hand from her mother's grasp and stared at her. "And where, pray tell, is the money to pay bills going to come from if I get fired? I have strict instructions to approve this project. I don't have a choice."

Della smiled smugly. "If you'll just calm down a minute and rein in that temper, I'll tell you."

"Mom—"

Della held up a hand to stop Kendall's protest. "For once in your life, just listen," she demanded. "I realize that I have been more of a burden than a help in the past, but then I didn't feel that *I* had much choice, and now I do. In two weeks I'll turn sixty. I'll be eligible for social security widow's benefits, and the extra money should help ease some of the financial burden you've been carrying. So you see, if you do lose your job and have to take one that doesn't pay as well, we should still be okay. Since I'm feeling better, you won't have to spend as much time taking care of me, and you might even seriously consider taking a part-time job. That way, with the help of a student loan, you could go back and finish your degree.''

Kendall was stunned. ''I—I don't know what to say.''

Della grinned and tweaked Kendall's cheek. ''Just say you'll at least think about it. Now, come along, dear, and I'll set up your tape recorder so that you can dictate your report.'' She took Kendall by the arm and pulled her toward the doorway. ''Just don't take too long, because Desiree promised to show me how she blends that special tea she sells at that swamp-tour gift shop. She claims she can make love potions, too, but I'm not so sure I believe in that kind of stuff.''

For long moments after her mother left her at Remy's desk, Kendall simply stared at the small tape recorder sitting in front of her. For the first time in years, she allowed herself to feel a glimmer of excitement. It was certainly a relief to know that she would no longer have the sole responsibility of carrying their financial burden, but even more exciting was the fact that her mother was actually looking ahead to the future and making plans. Kendall had no illusions about miracle cures, but if attitude counted for anything, surely that was half the battle?

*Well, it's now or never,* she thought, swinging her attention back to the problem of her report. But each time she reached for the tape recorder, her hand froze in midair. Bits and pieces of the past week flitted through her mind: images of the rich wetland with its moss-ladened trees, swirling dark waters, glorious birds and flowers, and a wealth of wildlife; Desiree and her patients, who like generations before them lived and thrived off the land; Claudia, the tour guides, the tourists; and Remy, always Remy, a larger-than-life presence who haunted her heart.

As had happened each time she'd thought of him during the past two days, tears stung her eyes. He was a man of principle and integrity whose emotions ran as deep as the murky waters of the bayou, a man who would always protect those he loved and that which he valued. "Even at the risk of his own life," she murmured.

Kendall went very still, not daring to breathe as, from out of nowhere, she suddenly recalled something Remy had said. *I don't have all of the answers yet...but now that I know for sure who tried to murder you, I will have them, just as soon as I catch the son of a bitch.*

The shock of the memory hit her full force. He hadn't gone after T-boy just to catch a poacher. He'd gone because of her, to insure her safety, as well.

The proof of his love had been right in front of her, but she'd been too blind and too self-absorbed to see it. Only love could make a man do what he'd set out to do.

With hot tears falling freely and a prayer on her lips for Remy's safe return, Kendall reached out, picked up the tape recorder and switched it on.

LATER THAT EVENING, in a remote section of the swamp, Remy crouched behind a stand of cypress and waited, trying to ignore the mosquitoes that swarmed around him like miniature vampires. In a clearing just ahead of him, a small fire crackled and burned, and huddled close to it was T-boy Melancon.

Remy still cursed himself each time he thought about how T-boy had given him the slip at the Landrys' fishing camp. He'd expected the bastard to show himself after Flora left. And like a fool, Remy had waited well into the evening before he'd realized that no lights were burning in the fishing shack and that T-boy had most likely opted to flee on foot. Remy had spotted fresh tracks near one of the back windows, and it had taken him two days of playing a deadly game of hide-and-seek through the swamp before he finally caught up with the poacher. And all the while, thoughts of Kendall kept swirling through his head. Would she be there when he finally got back? Or would she have given up on him and left?

Remy reached up and fingered the grip of the Glock in his shoulder holster. Each time he thought about T-boy bashing in Kendall's head and leaving her for dead, an unholy rage tore at his insides. Remy's fingers tightened on the grip. It would be so easy to put a bullet through the lowlife's head and be done with him. No trial, no chance for an acquittal on technicalities, and best of all, there would be no witnesses so no one would ever have to know. No one but him...

Even as Remy pulled out his weapon, he remembered the oath he'd taken so many years ago to uphold the law. Others had taken it and broken it, but he couldn't.

If he did he would be no better than them. His

hand tightened on the grip of his gun. In all the years he'd been an officer, he'd never broken the oath, and even though it had been four years since he'd quit the force, no matter how much he wanted to, he couldn't ignore it now. On this one, he'd have to trust Jake Trahan and hope that his newfound trust in the sheriff wasn't misplaced.

Remy glared at T-boy, and as the rage inside him slowly died, he knew he wouldn't shoot T-boy Melancon. He'd bring him in.

As silently as a stalking panther, Remy moved closer. When he saw T-boy suddenly stiffen and glance around, he knew that the time to show himself was at hand.

Remy stepped out from behind a tree. "On your feet and hands over your head," he demanded.

With his hands in the air, the poacher slowly rose to his feet and faced Remy. "What you gonna do, rich boy?" T-boy sneered. "Shoot me?"

"Don't tempt me," Remy answered, stepping closer. With his free hand he fished out a pair of handcuffs he'd stuck in his back pocket. "What I'm going to do is turn you over to Jake Trahan. With your record, attempted murder should put you away for a long, long time."

In the glow of the fire, Remy saw fear flicker in the older man's eyes. Fear made desperate men do crazy things, and the sooner he was handcuffed, the better Remy would feel.

He reached for the poacher's wrist. With no regard for the gun and in a move Remy hadn't expected, T-boy grabbed his gun hand and lunged at him. It was then that Remy realized he'd underestimated the older man's desperation and strength. When they hit the ground, they rolled and twisted, both fighting for control of the weapon. The poacher was wiry and quick for his age, and only by sheer determination and will was Remy able to finally subdue him and cuff him.

He jerked T-boy to his feet and pushed him ahead of him. "Get going," he growled. "I've wasted enough time and energy on you."

## CHAPTER FIFTEEN

ON THE FOLLOWING Monday morning, Kendall wasn't at all surprised when her boss, Don Talbot, called her into his office. She'd expected it, and one look at the thunderous expression on his face was all it took to confirm her suspicions. He barely gave her time to shut the door before he snatched a folder off his desk and shook it at her.

"What's the meaning of this?"

Kendall immediately recognized the folder and didn't bother with denial or pretense. She lifted her chin. "What part of my report don't you understand?" she asked pointedly.

His face grew red and blotchy with anger. "How dare you—"

Kendall stalked toward him. "No!" she interrupted, pointing an accusing finger at him. "How dare *you?* You've been entrusted by the taxpayers of this state with the responsibility of protecting its environment, and instead, you've sold out to the highest bidder. Well, I won't be a part of it any longer. Approving this would make me just as dirty and self-serving as you are."

He narrowed his eyes. "You're damn right you won't be a part of it any longer. You're fired!"

Kendall raised her chin, did an about-face and

stalked to the door, where she paused. "Oh, just one thing before I go." She turned to face him again. "A copy of the full assessment has been faxed to the governor, to the *Morning Advocate* and to the *Times-Picayune,* so don't think about trying to change one word of it to suit your purposes."

Don Talbot paled and the folder slid through his fingers, the papers spilling out and scattering onto his desk like falling leaves. "Get out!" he croaked. "Get out or I'll call security."

Kendall smiled, pivoted on her heels, then took enormous pleasure in slamming the door behind her as she left.

MILES AWAY in Bayou Beltane, Philip Delacroix pored over the updated figures his contractor had given him on the housing development. He'd taken the morning off and stayed home because he didn't want the constant interruptions he had to contend with at the office. With Desiree Boudreaux and that young pup, Remy, holding the old hag's so-called deed over his head, it was more urgent than ever to get the ball rolling. When the phone on his desk rang, he ignored it and let the answering machine monitor the call.

But the moment he heard Don Talbot's voice, Philip snatched up the receiver. Finally, he thought. He was finally going to get the news he'd been waiting for. But the longer he listened to what Talbot was telling him, the tighter he clenched the receiver.

"What the hell do you mean, it's been turned down?" He exploded out of his chair. "I don't want to hear any of your goddamn excuses.... An investigation?'' His fist crashed against the desktop. "Listen here, you son of a bitch. If I go down, so do you. If there's an injunction, I'll fight it, and if you know what's good for you, you'll cooperate—you'll back me one hundred per cent or I'll ruin you.''

Philip slammed the receiver onto the phone, then fell back in his chair. Visions of ugly gris-gris flashed in his head, and a shiver of fear ran up his spine. He should have known something like this would happen. It was all that bitch Flora's fault, her and her evil voodoo dolls. And now there would be all hell to pay.

His face twisted in rage.

INTERSTATE TRAFFIC in Baton Rouge was heavier than usual. By the time Kendall reached the I-12 exit her euphoria at having had the last word had long since faded and the bite of reality was slowly sinking in.

Worry for Remy consumed her, making her impatient with the slow-moving traffic. There had been no answer at his houseboat or at Desiree's home any of the times she'd phoned, and her imagination was running wild with speculation. Had Remy succeeded in apprehending T-boy? Would he be home when she returned? Or even now was he lying in a hospital close to death, or worse…? Kendall didn't want to think about worse.

The hour-and-a-half drive from Baton Rouge to Bayou Beltane seemed to take forever. It was awkward driving with the use of only one arm, and her left one at that, but she managed, grateful as never before for automatic transmission.

By the time she finally pulled into the parking lot of the gift shop, her shoulders were aching and her stomach was tied in knots of apprehension. To her disappointment, it was Claudia's day off, and since Kendall didn't know the man who was taking Claudia's place, she didn't feel comfortable asking him questions about Remy.

Now, if she could just find someone to take her to the houseboat, she thought, eyeing the line of tourists boarding one of the tour boats docked at the pier. Maybe one of Remy's guides would take her.

The name of the guide she talked to was Ray, and when she explained that she was a friend of Remy's and needed a ride to his houseboat, he was more than happy to help out.

"Anything for the boss man," he replied. "It will take a little while, but the tour goes pretty close to his place, and I could just drop you off."

Kendall was tired and worried, and under the cast her arm was beginning to itch in the unseasonable heat. Having to crowd onto the boat with a bunch of strangers and listen to the guide's spiel about the wetland, no matter how informative, was the last thing she felt like doing, but she figured she had little choice.

When she finally spotted the houseboat thirty minutes later, her heartbeat quickened. Hoping and praying that Remy's boat would be moored at the pier, she squinted against the glare of the midday sun. When she finally spotted the familiar boat, a cry of relief broke from her lips.

With the ease of an expert captain, Ray slid the

big boat up beside the pier so Kendall could climb out.

"Thanks, Ray," she called out as he pulled away from the pier.

With a jaunty wave, he put the motor in gear and resumed the tour.

Should she simply walk in? Kendall wondered as she cautiously approached the kitchen entrance. Or should she knock? She had just raised her fist to knock, her insides quivering in anticipation, when the door abruptly swung open.

The sight of Remy sent her blood joyously racing through her veins. But her elation was short-lived when she saw the wary expression on his face and noted his disheveled appearance. He was wearing a pair of dirty jeans and a grimy looking T-shirt, and he badly needed a shave. His eyes were red-rimmed.

"Kendall?" His voice was thick and unsteady, and she tried to quell her growing unease when she saw his eyes narrow with suspicion.

"May I come in?"

"It is you!" He suddenly reached out and pulled her to him almost roughly. "I thought I was dreaming...or had finally gone mad."

"I—I don't understand," she gasped, finding it difficult to breathe in his vicelike grip.

But he didn't seem to hear her. "I don't care what you put in that report—write it any way you damn well please. Just don't ever leave me again."

It took Kendall only a moment to realize that something was amiss. "But I didn't leave you," she cried. "I mean, I did leave, but not like you think. Didn't Desiree or my mother tell you where I went?"

As suddenly as he'd grabbed her, Remy loosened his hold. Uncertainty was written all over his face as he held her at arm's length and stared into her eyes. "Now I don't understand," he said. "All I could get out of Desiree was that you had left, probably for good."

"Why would she say such a thing?"

Remy released her, shoved his fingers through his hair, then shook his head. "I'll be damned if I know, but you can bet I'm going to ask her next time I see her. The last few days have been hell."

On impulse, Kendall reached up and caressed his jaw. After days of worrying whether he was alive or dead, it felt so good to be able to touch him. "I'm sorry," she whispered. "I did try to call."

A dark flush stole across his jaw. "I tried to call you, too, when I first got back Friday night, and after about the tenth time, I..." He winced, as if what he was saying was painful. "I was so angry and frustrated that I threw the phone into the bayou. After what Desiree had said, I figured I had lost you for good." He covered her hand with his, and when he brought it to his lips and kissed her palm, shivers of awareness shot up her arm. "Where *have* you been?" he asked.

Kendall leveled a steady gaze at him. "I went to Baton Rouge and filed my report. On Friday night, until the wee hours of Saturday morning, I was at the office typing it up, because I didn't trust anyone else to do it for me. And believe me, it wasn't easy with this cast."

His hand tightened on hers and his eyes grew cool. "And?"

"And I rejected the project. I'm ashamed that I ever considered approving it to begin with."

"Why...what changed your mind?"

Kendall swallowed hard. "Lots of things, but ultimately, it was you," she said softly. "It was your unselfish love for the swamp, its wildlife and its people, that finally made me see how wrong I've been. I finally realized that trying to hang on to a job in this situation would be just as self-serving as what the man I worked for was doing."

Remy tilted his head. "Worked? As in past tense?"

"He fired me." Kendall gave a little shrug. "I'm officially unemployed. You wouldn't happen to need an extra tour guide, would you?"

Kendall had been half teasing, but Remy's sudden, stern-faced expression sobered her instantly. "What I need," he said evenly, "is you."

For long moments his words seemed to hang in the air between them, then they both spoke at once.

"Remy, I—"

"Kendall, I—"

"Love you." They said the last words together, then he pulled her into his arms and held her so close that she could feel his heart beating in perfect rhythm with hers.

He loved her. He really loved her, Kendall realized in amazement. She'd known it, deep in her heart of hearts, and she'd told herself she didn't need the actual words, but hearing them was like the sound of a glorious symphony that played for her alone.

"I never thought I would say those words ever

again," he murmured. "Until now...until you came into my life."

His confession was a double-edged sword that pierced Kendall's soul. He was thinking of the woman named Julie, the woman he'd loved and lost, and while his profession of love filled Kendall's heart to overflowing, she couldn't help the momentary stab of jealousy she felt.

"She must have been a very special lady," she whispered haltingly.

Remy didn't pretend to misunderstand. "Julie was a special lady," he murmured as he pressed Kendall's head against his chest and nuzzled her hair. "But what was between us happened in another lifetime. For a while after she was killed I didn't give a damn about anything or anyone. All of those things I had believed in—my job, my fellow officers, justice for all—turned out to be an illusion. The reality involved dirty cops and corruption all the way to the top, and I found that I couldn't deal with it. There's an old saying that you can't fight city hall, but I had to find that out the hard way."

Remy paused and took a deep breath. "Then one day," he continued, his tone growing less somber, "I found this injured lady on Willow Island, and nothing in my life has been the same since."

Kendall smiled, more secure with each passing minute that he truly loved her. "Mine hasn't been exactly a bed of roses," she quipped, "not with thorns like T-boy...." She suddenly pushed herself out of Remy's arms and glowered up at him. "Speaking of pricks, did you track him down?"

Amusement danced in Remy's eyes. "Right now

I'd rather not talk about T-boy Melancon. Suffice it to say he won't be bothering you or anyone for a long time. In fact—'' a wolfish grin spread on his face ''—I don't think I want to talk at all. I'd much rather do other things.''

Before she could protest, he reached down, scooped her up in his arms and carried her inside, straight to the bedroom, where he deposited her on the bed. Slowly, he stripped away each article of her clothing, and by the time he removed the last piece, she no longer wanted to protest.

Then he began his own striptease, starting with the T-shirt and ending with the grimy jeans. The sight of him standing before her in all of his virile, raw beauty robbed her of any coherent thoughts as love mingled with desire and pulsed through her veins.

When he reached for her, the trembling in his hands reflected a vulnerability that she knew was rare for a man like Remy.

"I love you, Kendall Delaney." His voice was hoarse and rough. "My very own, sweet Jane Doe," he murmured. "My beautiful brown-eyed lady. With all of my heart and soul, I love you."

His declaration was humbling, a memory she would cherish for the rest of her life. Tears sprang to her eyes and a knot of emotion lodged in her throat. "I love you, Remy Delacroix, now and forever."

Then she was in his arms, his lips devouring hers. His rough hands caressed and played her body ever so tenderly as if it were a rare, exquisite instrument and he was the maestro, coaxing yet demanding everything she had to give. Each touch, each caress made her blood sing, and Kendall knew that she had found her other half, her soul mate for life.

IT WAS LATE AFTERNOON before either Kendall or Remy thought of getting out of bed. But the sound of an approaching outboard motor had Kendall groaning and Remy cursing as they scrambled for clothes.

Since Remy was the first dressed, he was the one who answered the knock at the kitchen door. By the time Kendall entered the kitchen, he was still trying to get rid of Jake Trahan.

"I just need you to clear up a few details about T-boy," Jake insisted. "Besides, I could sure use a cup of coffee."

Remy had just opened his mouth to protest when he heard yet another boat approaching. "What is this?" he grumbled. "Open house?" He stepped past Jake and glared at the boat docking at his pier. Seated in it were Desiree and Kendall's mother.

"Aw, hell!" Remy muttered, gesturing for the sheriff to enter. "You might as well come in."

Della was on his heels, nodding and smiling at Remy before going inside. Desiree followed more slowly, but when she reached Remy, she paused. Her old eyes narrowed in speculation as she scrutinized him from head to toe.

"From the looks of you, I'd say that your woman decided to return."

Remy glowered at the old woman. "You knew she was coming back, so why did you lie to me?"

A slow, self-satisfied smile spread across her wrinkled face. "There's an old saying that you don't miss your water until the well runs dry." She reached up and patted his jaw. "Slow learners need help—a little push once in a while to realize what they really feel."

As Remy watched the old woman glide past him and disappear through the kitchen door, he was so furious that at first he didn't trust himself to move. She'd done it on purpose! She and Kendall's mother had purposely conspired together and played matchmakers. Slowly the anger drained out of him. He didn't like being manipulated, but how could he honestly object when the end result was Kendall's love?

Inside the kitchen, Jake was apologizing to Kendall. "Sorry for the intrusion, ma'am, but I was out of town when Remy brought in T-boy, and there's a few loose ends I need to tie up."

"Don't mind me," Kendall said, sliding a glance at Remy as he entered. "I've been wanting to hear about this, anyway."

"Me, too," echoed Desiree.

Della nodded in agreement. "Yes, do tell us all about it, Remy."

One glance at the expectant faces staring at him, and he let out a long-suffering sigh. "Okay, might as well get this over with once and for all." He threw Kendall a hopeless look. "I guess now is as good a time as any." He gestured for all of them to be seated. Jake brought out a mini tape recorder and set it in front of Remy. And while Kendall brewed a pot of coffee and served it, Remy once again recounted the harrowing two days he'd spent in the swamp chasing T-boy Melancon.

When he'd finished, Jake switched off the tape re-

corder, pocketed the tiny machine, then stood.
"Good enough," he said, his gaze focused on Remy.
"But next time, check with me before you go chasing off into the swamp, and if you ever decide to go back into law enforcement, be sure and give me a call."

Remy held the other man's gaze, then slowly nodded. "I'll keep it in mind."

Jake shrugged. "I'll need you to drop by the station and sign a statement, say tomorrow afternoon?"

"Yeah, I'll be by," Remy answered.

Jake turned his attention to Kendall, who had sat down next to Remy. "I'll need a statement from you, too, ma'am. If you can come in, I'll get a lineup together so that you can identify T-boy as the one who assaulted you."

Kendall nodded, but not before Remy saw a glint of fear flash in her eyes. Without a thought as to how his action would be interpreted, he reached over, covered her hand with his and squeezed. "Kendall, honey, will that be a problem?"

She turned her hand in his and laced their fingers together. "No problem. Like I told you after what I thought was my nightmare, I'd recognize that face anywhere."

Remy nodded, then turned back to Jake. "I'll bring her with me when I come."

Jake left first, but it took another thirty minutes before Desiree and Kendall's mother finally decided it was time to go.

Remy helped Della into the boat, but when he turned to lend a supporting arm to Desiree, the old woman beckoned him aside.

In a voice so low that he had to strain his ears to hear, she said, "I wanted to thank you for not involving Flora, and I also wanted you to know that she won't be bothering your woman again."

On impulse, Remy leaned over and kissed the old woman's cheek. "You're welcome," he whispered.

As Desiree's boat disappeared around the bend in the bayou, Remy and Kendall stood arm in arm on the dock. Kendall leaned her head against Remy's shoulder. "My mother looks better than I've seen her look in years. Whatever Desiree is doing must be working." Kendall suddenly grimaced. "For a minute there, I didn't think they were going to leave, but I'm glad they did. I'm also glad Desiree insisted that my mother spend some more time with her. I'm not quite ready to tell my mother about losing my job—not yet, anyway."

Remy chuckled, recalling the expression on Della's face when Desiree had taken her by the arm and firmly led her to the door. "Desiree can be pretty persuasive when she has to be." He turned to Kendall and cupped her face. "Speaking of jobs, I heard of an opening you might be interested in."

Kendall frowned. "If you're referring to that remark I made about you hiring me as one of your guides, I was just joking. I'm hoping that now I can finally go back to school and finish my degree."

Remy shook his head. "That's not quite the job I had in mind, and you can still go back to school if that's what you want. But there's this man I know who is desperate for a wife, someone he can spend the rest of his life with. The job doesn't pay much, just his undying love and devotion and a promise to always care for you. Think you would be interested?"

For long moments, Kendall simply stared at him with a look in her eyes that spoke volumes. It was the look of love that Remy knew he'd never tire of seeing, and as the sun dipped below the moss-ladened cypress on the edge of the swamp, Kendall finally whispered, "When do I start?"

# DELTA JUSTICE

continues with

## *IN THE BRIDE'S DEFENSE*

### *by Kelsey Roberts*

Marie Delacroix never meant to kill anyone
with her herbal treatments, and medical
examiner Lucas Henderson believed her.
But Delta justice could be swift and brutal;
without proof of her innocence she didn't
stand a chance. And the only way Lucas
and Marie could get proof was to pose as
man and wife…

**Available in December**

**Here's a preview!**

# *CHAPTER ONE*

"AND I WAS AFRAID it was Charly who would be brain-damaged," Marie said as she pushed open the door to her apartment. "Obviously I should have been concerned about you."

"Will you please shut up and let me explain?"

"Explain what, Lucas?" Marie went to the cupboard, took out some herbal tea, then put the kettle on to boil.

He followed her and simply leaned his big body into her. She didn't dare move.

"I'm not real big on brute strength," she informed him.

"At least I finally got your attention," he said in a much less threatening tone.

"You certainly got my attention in the car. I'm simply going to attribute your proposal to a lapse in sanity on your part."

"Marie, calm down and hear me out. That's all I ask."

Marie struggled briefly, then gave up in quiet frustration. Her anger slowly subsided. She knew Lucas well enough to realize that he hadn't simply been toying with her emotions when he'd made his ridiculous proposal. "So, talk."

"I've narrowed the search down to Haven."

It took her brain a minute to switch gears. "You think someone at Haven was blackmailing David?"

"Possibly."

"So, we'll go up and interview—"

"I've tried that."

"You went up there?"

He shook his head.

"I've called. Haven prides itself on discretion. No interviews. No tours. The only way in is as a married couple."

"That's why you asked me to marry you?"

There was a flicker of emotion in his eyes that she didn't know how to read, but all he said was "I can't think of any other reason, can you?"

"We'll just tell them we're married," she suggested.

"We'd be required to produce a certificate in order to register."

"We'll forge one. I'm sure someone in my family can—"

"They're real sticklers at Haven," he explained. "Apparently they verify everything."

The struggle went out of her as she considered the possibility. "You would actually marry me just to get into Haven?"

"No. I'd marry you to find David's killer." His expression grew determined. "And to clear your name."

# LOOK FOR OUR FOUR FABULOUS MEN!

Each month some of today's bestselling authors bring
four new fabulous men to Harlequin American Romance.
Whether they're rebel ranchers, millionaire power brokers
or sexy single dads, they're all gallant princes—and
they're all ready to sweep you into lighthearted fantasies
and contemporary fairy tales where anything is possible
and where all your dreams come true!

You don't even have to make a wish...
Harlequin American Romance will grant your every desire!

Look for Harlequin American Romance
wherever Harlequin books are sold!

# HARLEQUIN®

## I N T R I G U E®

### *We'll leave you breathless!*

If you've been looking for thrilling tales of
contemporary passion and sensuous love stories
with taut, edge-of-the-seat suspense—
then you'll *love* **Harlequin Intrigue!**

Every month, you'll meet four new heroes
who are guaranteed to make your spine tingle
and your pulse pound. With them you'll enter
into the exciting world of Harlequin Intrigue—
where your life is on the line
and so is your heart!

## THAT'S INTRIGUE—DYNAMIC
## ROMANCE AT ITS BEST!

### HARLEQUIN®

## I N T R I G U E®

INT-GENR

# HARLEQUIN  PRESENTS®

**HARLEQUIN PRESENTS**
men you won't be able to resist
falling in love with...

**HARLEQUIN PRESENTS**
women who have feelings
just like your own...

**HARLEQUIN PRESENTS**
powerful passion in
exotic international settings...

**HARLEQUIN PRESENTS**
intense, dramatic stories that will keep you
turning to the very last page...

**HARLEQUIN PRESENTS**
The world's bestselling romance series!

## Harlequin Romance®

**D**elightful

**A**ffectionate

**R**omantic

**E**motional

**T**ender

**O**riginal

**D**aring

**R**iveting

**E**nchanting

**A**dventurous

**M**oving

Harlequin Romance—the
series that has it all!

HROM-G

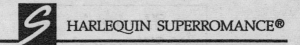

# HARLEQUIN SUPERROMANCE®

## ...there's more to the story!

Superromance. A *big* satisfying read about
unforgettable characters. Each month we offer
*four* very different stories that range from family
drama to adventure and mystery, from highly
emotional stories to romantic comedies—and
much more! Stories about people you'll
believe in and care about. Stories too
compelling to put down....

Our authors are among today's *best* romance
writers. You'll find familiar names and
talented newcomers. Many of them are
award winners—and you'll see why!

If you want the biggest and best
in romance fiction, you'll get it
from Superromance!

Available wherever Harlequin books are sold.

Look us up on-line at: http://www.romance.net

HS-GEN

**Harlequin® Historical**

From rugged lawmen and
valiant knights to defiant heiresses
and spirited frontierswomen,
Harlequin Historicals will
capture your imagination with
their dramatic scope, passion
and adventure.

Harlequin Historicals...
they're too good to miss!